HER COWBOY BILLIONAIRE BEST FRIEND

A WHITTAKER BROTHERS NOVEL, CHRISTMAS IN CORAL CANYON BOOK 1

LIZ ISAACSON

feel good fiction

LIANA JOHNSON

ISBN-13: 978-1718037731

CHAPTER 1

Graham Whittaker gazed at the Tetons, wishing just the tops of the mountains were snow-covered. Unfortunately, it hadn't stopped snowing for a few days, and the white stuff covered everything from the mountaintops to the grass outside the lodge he'd just bought and moved into over Christmas.

He liked to think heaven was weeping for the loss of his father, the same way the Whittaker family had been for the past nine days. With the funeral and burial two days past now, everyone had gone back to their normal lives—except Graham.

"This is your normal life now," he told himself as he turned away from what some probably considered a picturesque view of the country, the snow, the mountains.

Whiskey Mountain Lodge was a beautiful spot, nestled right up against the mountains on the west and the Teton

National park on the north. It had a dozen guest rooms and boasted all the amenities needed to keep them fed, entertained, and happy for days on end.

Not that it mattered. Graham wasn't planning on running the lodge as the quaint bed and breakfast in the mountains that it had previously been.

No, Whiskey Mountain Lodge was his new home.

His father had left behind an entire business that needed running, and Graham had nothing left for him in Seattle anyway. So he'd come to help his mother after the sudden death of her husband, and he'd had enough time to find somewhere to live and operate Springside Energy Operations as the CEO.

It was a step up, really. He'd only been the lead developer at Qualetics Robotics in Seattle, but the itch to develop technology and robotics to make people's lives easier had died when his father had.

Graham hoped it would come back; Springside could definitely benefit from having the first fracking robot to identify the natural gases under the surface of the Earth *before* they drilled. But they were years away from that.

Just like Graham felt years away from anyone else out here.

A dog barked, reminding him that he'd inherited his father's dog as well as his company, and he went over to the back door to let Bear back in. The big black lab seemed to move quite slowly, though he still wore his usual smile on his face.

"Hey, Bear." He scrubbed the dog to wipe off the

snowflakes that had settled on his back. "Guess I better go check on the horses."

Whiskey Mountain had come with a riding stable, something tourists apparently liked to do in the summer months in Wyoming. Graham had grown up in Coral Canyon, Wyoming, but his parents lived in town, in a normal house, without any horses.

Of course, every man in Wyoming learned to ride, and Graham and his three brothers were no exception. But it had been a very, very long time since he'd saddled up in any sense of the word.

But today, though the lodge was a huge building, with dozens of places to which he could escape, he felt trapped. So he plucked his hat from the peg by the door and positioned it on his head. He didn't get many opportunities to wear a cowboy hat in Seattle, but here, he'd worn it every day. And he liked it.

The brim kept the snow off his face as he trudged down the path he'd shoveled every day since moving in and headed toward the stables.

The stables were named DJ Riders, and Graham had no idea where it had come from. There were only three horses that had come with the property, and thankfully, the loft held enough hay to keep them fed for a while.

Graham went through the motions of feeding them, cleaning out their stalls, and making sure they had fresh water that hadn't frozen over. January in Wyoming wasn't for the weak-hearted, that was for sure, horse or human.

The chores done, Graham closed up the stables but turned away from the lodge up the lane. He had plenty of unpacking to do and no inclination to do it. Besides, it would keep, as he'd been living in the lodge for three days without the family pictures, all the dishes, or more than one towel. He'd survived so far, thanks to a four-wheel-drive vehicle and a pocketful of cash.

He wandered away from the stables, the barn, the rest of the outbuildings of the lodge. He passed a gazebo he hadn't even known existed until that very moment, and he wondered what else he'd find on this parcel of land he'd put his name on. And who knew what spring would bring?

Probably pollen and allergies, he thought, still not entirely happy to be back in Coral Canyon though he'd made the decision to leave his job in Seattle and settle back in his hometown.

The snow muted his footsteps and made it difficult to go very far very fast. Didn't matter. He had the whole day to do whatever he wanted. Tomorrow too. It wasn't until Monday that he'd have to put on a suit and start figuring out how to manage an energy company with over two hundred employees.

He approached another building, this one a bit different than the ones he'd seen before. He wasn't sure what it was, though it looked like a small cabin, with a stovepipe sticking out of the shingles on the roof. Did the lodge have a smaller place to live? Was this another guest area he could rent out?

He stepped closer and peered in the window, not seeing a door anywhere. The place was simply furnished and appeared to be one room with a door leading out of it on his right and into what he assumed was a bedroom.

A woman came out of the bedroom, buttoning her coat. Graham yelped and backed up at the same time a dog put his front paws on the windowsill inside the house and started barking. And barking. And barking.

With his heart pounding and his adrenaline spiking out of control, Graham's brain didn't seem to be working properly. Therefore, he couldn't move. Didn't even think to move.

So he was still standing there like a peeping Tom when the woman lifted the window and said, "What are you doing here?" in a tone of voice that could've frozen the water into snow if the temperature hadn't already done it.

"I—I—" Graham stammered. "Who are you?"

She cocked her hip, and Graham noticed the long, honey-blonde hair as she threw it over her shoulder before folding her arms. She possessed a pretty face, with a sprinkling of freckles across her cheeks and nose. Her eyes could've been any color, as he was looking from the outside in and the light wasn't the same.

If he'd had to, he'd categorize them as dangerous, especially when they flashed lightning at him.

"I am the owner of this property," she said. "And you're trespassing."

Graham frowned, but at least his brain had started operating normally again. It was his pulse that was galloping now, wondering what he had to do to get invited in to find out what color those eyes were.

"Oh," he said. "I'm sorry. I thought this was my place. I

just bought Whiskey Mountain Lodge." He waved in the general direction of the lodge, hoping it was the right way.

"The border is back there about a hundred yards," she said, still positioned like he might come at her through the window screen. "There's a fence."

"Maybe it's buried in all the snow." Because he had definitely not crossed a fence line. He might have become a city slicker but he still knew what a fence meant. "I'm Graham Whittaker."

A noise halfway between a squeak and a meow came from her mouth. Those eyes rounded, but he still couldn't tell what color they were. "Graham Whittaker?"

He tilted his head now, studying her. Because she knew him. No one spoke with that much surprise in their voice if they didn't know a person.

"Yes," he said slowly. "I'm...." He didn't know how to finish. Everyone in Coral Canyon knew his father had died. Everyone knew the Whittakers had come to mourn. He supposed everyone thought they'd all left again, except for his mother and his youngest brother, Beau, who lived in town and worked as a lawyer.

But he didn't know what he was still doing in Coral Canyon, or why he felt the urge to explain it to this woman.

"Just a second." She slammed the window shut and moved away. Feeling stupid, Graham stood there in the snow, wondering what she was going to do. Half a minute later, the dog that had tried to rip his face off through the glass came bounding through the snow from the front of the house.

"Clearwater," the woman called after him, but the dog was either disobedient or didn't care. The blue heeler came right up to Graham and started sniffing him.

Graham chuckled and scratched the dog behind his ears. "Yeah, I've got a lab. You can probably smell 'im. Bear? His name's Bear."

The blonde woman came around the corner of the cabin, and she stopped much further away than her dog had. "Graham Whittaker." This time she didn't phrase it as a question, and a hint of a smile touched her lips. "You don't remember me, do you?"

Graham abandoned his administrations to the dog and took a step toward her, trying to place her. He thought he'd definitely remember someone as shapely as her, what with those long legs that curved into hips and narrowed to a waist, even in the black jacket she'd buttoned around herself.

He was about to apologize when the answer hit him full in the chest. "Laney Boyd?" He tore his eyes from hers to glance around the land, not that he could tell anything with the piles and piles of snow.

"Is this Echo Ridge Ranch?" he asked. He hadn't realized the lodge property butted up against the ranch where he'd spent time as a teenager. And without looking back at Laney, he knew he'd find a pair of light green eyes. Eyes that came to life when she was atop a horse. Eyes that had always called to him. Eyes that saw more than he'd ever wanted her to. Beautiful, light green eyes he wanted to get to experience again.

When he looked at her again, her grin had filled her

whole face. "It's Laney McAllister now," she said, dashing every hope he had of rekindling an old friendship—and maybe making it into something more.

Which is stupid, he told himself as he chuckled and walked through the snow to give her a hug hello. *You just got your heart broken. No need to do it again.*

CHAPTER 2

L aney McAllister shook her head as she laughed, the sound more incredulous than happy. She couldn't believe Graham Whittaker had returned to Coral Canyon. Could *not* believe it. The man was twice as broad as he'd been as an eighteen-year-old, his voice twice as deep, his charisma twice as strong.

Her heart leapt and flopped and bounced around as he drew her against his chest and said, "It's so good to see you again." He released her quickly, and she put an extra step of distance between them, the moment suddenly awkward.

"You runnin' the ranch?" he asked.

"Ever since Dad died." And of course, that was why he'd come home too. His father had just passed away, and someone needed to manage the fracking operation that had made the Whittakers one of the wealthiest families in Wyoming.

Pain pinched between his eyes, and Laney wished she could take back her words. She understood the pain of losing a parent so young, and she reached out and put her hand on Graham's forearm. Even through the layers of his coat, a charge passed between them.

It wasn't the first time she'd felt this pulse between them, but it had always been one-sided. Graham had dated the same girl all through high school, and then he'd left for college. Left Emma Darrow here to marry someone else. Left his family to pursue some sort of computer science in the technology hub of the country a few states away. Left Laney, his best friend who'd always encouraged him to do what made him happy.

Now, looking at the strong lines of his face, that cowboy hat that made him rugged and sexy, and those beautiful brown eyes, she could tell he was not happy. Maybe two decades had gone by since they'd truly been in touch—social media and a quick card of condolences when her father had died didn't count—but Laney had known Graham as well as she'd known herself. They'd been best friends for twelve years before they'd graduated and he'd gone to MIT and she'd gone to a university in Cheyenne.

Their lives had taken divergent paths since then, and yet, there he stood. Right in front of her. Looking every bit as vulnerable and handsome and powerful as she remembered.

"I'm sorry about your father." Her voice lifted into the air, barely loud enough for her to hear among the silencing snow and whispering wind.

Graham nodded, his bearded jaw tightening. *The beard's*

new, Laney thought. It wasn't very long and the gray that dotted it only reminded her of how many years had passed since she'd seen him last.

"Do you want to come in?" she asked, indicating the cabin. "It's freezing out here." She'd been about to head over to the stables to take care of her horses, but they could wait a few more minutes for their breakfast. And Bailey—

The thought of her daughter hit her like a punch to the chest. Then she remembered that Bailey had spent the night at her mother's and wouldn't be home until late afternoon.

"I think I'll pass." Graham tipped his hat at her. "I don't want your husband to get the wrong idea about us." His dark eyes bored into hers, and the truth bubbled to the back of her throat.

"My husband lives somewhere in the South," she said. "And he's an ex." She cinched her arms across her chest, the emotions that went with her divorce still so close to the surface.

Shock crossed his face. "I'm sorry. I didn't know." A smile touched his lips and as she dropped her hand from his arm, he caught it in his. A squeeze. A nod. That smile.

Oh, boy. That smile did dangerous things to her stomach.

He released her hand half a second before she was going to shake his away. Not that she didn't want to hold his hand. She did. But she didn't need his sympathy. Not over Mike.

"It's been three years. We're managing okay." She took

a deep breath—a big mistake what with the sub-arctic temperatures that froze the inside of her nose.

"We?" Though he looked away, back toward his lodge, the curiosity in his voice filled the sky surrounding them.

He'd find out anyway. Coral Canyon was a small town, even if her and Bailey living up at Echo Ridge wasn't new gossip. And Laney wasn't embarrassed about anything anymore.

"Me and my daughter," she said. "Bailey's six."

"Oh." He brought his eyes back to hers. "Where is she now?"

"At my mother's. That's why I was...." She trailed off, the thought of sharing something personal with Graham a little too much to expect at the moment. She'd heard he was back for the funeral, of course. She had no idea he'd been planning to stay.

And while they'd known each other well in high school, that was well, high school. He was thirty-nine now, and she'd be thirty-nine in March.

"Do you come out here a lot when Bailey's gone?" he asked.

"Sometimes," she said. "It's nice to get away." And she rarely had the opportunity to do so. Bailey had a lot of chores, and she did most of them without complaint. But she was still only six and needed constant looking after, as did their four dogs, two cats, and thirteen horses.

"I know what you mean." Graham gazed up through the bare branches of the trees beside the cabin and then flashed her a smile that seemed too tight around the edges. "Want me to walk you back to your place?"

"Oh, I'm fine." She waved away his offer, regretting it as soon as her hand fell back to her side.

"Can I get your number?" he asked.

Their gazes locked, and Laney's heart did a weird pittering pattering pulsing in her chest.

"I've been living in the city for a while," he said with a chuckle. "I'm glad to know you're so close. Would you mind if I called you from time to time if I need help?"

She couldn't imagine a single thing the tall, dark, handsome, and rich Graham couldn't figure out on his own, but she pulled out her phone and said, "What's your number?"

He dictated it to her and she sent him three smiley face emoticons. "Now you have my number." She grinned as his phone chimed and he pulled it from his back pocket. Just watching him tap and swipe with that little smirk on his face got her blood heating.

"Well, I have to get to work," she said. "My horses can't feed themselves."

"It would be nice if they could, wouldn't it?" He laughed, the sound delicious to all of her senses.

"How many horses do you have?" she asked, stepping toward the road that led back to the epicenter of the ranch.

"Just the three," he said. "You?"

"Thirteen." They reached the road in front of the cabin, Clearwater at their heels. She pointed south. "Your place is just up there and around the curve." She faced northeast. "I'm down this way."

He let his gaze linger down the road toward Echo Ridge and then said, "Good to see you again, Laney," before turning south and walking down the road. She watched him for too long, but his long, jean-clad legs with those broad shoulders clothed in black leather...he had grown into positively the most beautiful man she'd ever known.

And he'd been gorgeous as a teenager. It almost didn't seem fair.

Sighing, she turned away and reminded herself that she already had enough to do, dozens of tasks to keep her busy. She didn't need to add a man to the list. Oh, no siree. She did not.

———

EXACTLY THIRTY HOURS HAD PASSED BEFORE GRAHAM'S NAME brightened her phone screen. She flipped the two hamburgers she was frying for lunch before swiping open the call. She eyed Bailey, sitting at the kitchen counter with a coloring book in front of her as she said, "Hey."

"Hey." Graham sounded like he had a smile on his face. "I'm wondering what you know about dermatitis in horses."

Laney laid a slice of cheese on each hamburger patty. "What makes you think your horses have dermatitis?"

"I looked it up on my phone."

"What does it say to do?"

"I have no idea. There's no treatment. I also don't know how it happened. Can you come take a look at the horses?" He spoke in a tone that didn't really allow her to say no.

She wondered if anyone ever told him no, and what he'd do if they did.

As if Laney didn't have enough to do. But she said, "Sure," anyway, and said, "I have to go." She hung up before she could give away too many of her irrational and confusing feelings. They'd kept her awake much too long last night as it was, and she couldn't give them more stage time in her mind during the day too.

"Here you go, Bay," she said, scooping the hamburgers out of the pan. "Time for lunch. Put those away."

The strawberry-blonde child began putting her crayons back in the box. "Is there avocados?"

"Not today." Laney smiled at her daughter and added, "But I have tomatoes and lettuce, and the burgers have cheese on them." She put a bun on Bailey's plate. "Make it how you like it."

Laney pulled out a bag of chips they'd partially eaten last week and set them on the counter too. They'd gone into town for church that morning, but she hadn't seen Graham. His mother was there, as was Beau, but Graham didn't sit with them. She hadn't seen any tire tracks leading from the lodge either, and she wondered if he'd stay holed up at Whiskey Mountain Lodge to work, or if he'd take over his father's office in the small building Springside Energy operated out of.

Why Graham Whittaker took up so much of her brainpower was a mystery to her. Frustrating, too. So she banished him as she put mustard, mayo, and ketchup on her bun, added lettuce and tomato and bit into her burger.

"You're coming out to the barn with me," she reminded

Bailey as they finished their lunch. "You've got to check on the cats, remember? And the outdoor dogs. And make sure all the chickens have enough feed and water."

"Okay." Bailey only ate a few bites of her burger but plenty of chips. Laney probably should've argued with her about it, but she didn't have the energy today.

She thought of Mike, of where he might be and what he might be doing. No matter what it was, it wasn't dealing with the bills of a ranch that made marginally more than it needed to run, or his daughter's dietary needs.

"School on Monday," she added, as if Bailey had forgotten from the last time Laney had told her. "Back to real life."

"I like Christmas break," Bailey said, a frown pulling at her eyebrows.

"Me too." She ruffled Bailey's hair and put her plate in the sink. "Get suited up. It's cold out there." She stepped over to the back door and pulled on her own boots, then her coat, hat, and scarf. "I'm going to be checking on the cattle today. Stay in the barn when you're done with your chores, okay?"

Bailey agreed, and Laney helped her with her coat and scarf, making sure her daughter wouldn't get frostbite when they went outside.

She pulled her gloves on last and they stepped into the winter weather. The snow had stopped, and the sky was blue and clear. But the sun shining on the landscape only made things bright, not warm. In fact, it was even colder now that the cloud cover had moved on.

Their breath steamed in front of them as they made the trek across the back lawn and into the barns and stables.

"Cats," Laney reminded Bailey. "Dogs. Chickens."

"Cats, dogs, chickens," Bailey recited back, and she got to work with the two cats she'd named herself. Laney watched her feed KC, short for Kitty Cat, and Meow, the two stray cats Bailey had kept in her bedroom until Laney had smelled them.

With everything else they'd lost, she couldn't make Bailey get rid of them, so they'd compromised. They could be barn cats, catching mice and running around the ranch. But they simply couldn't stay in the house.

Laney only let two of the dogs in as it was, and she glanced over to the outdoor mutts—Georgia and Savannah —on her way toward the back of the barn. She loved her ranching life, she really did. But some days, especially in the dead of winter, she wondered what it would be like to have a husband who went out in the cold and took care of the chores while she stayed inside and sipped tea and baked cookies.

Not that she was the tea-drinking cookie-baking type of woman. But she knew some women who were, and she never felt like she fit in with them. That, combined with living so far out of town, meant most of her conversations happened with Bailey or a bovine. Her gaze wandered to the south as soon as she stepped outside, but she couldn't see even an inkling of the lodge from her property.

It sat up the hill, but then down in a swell, and the only time she even knew it was there was when she drove by to go to town. Still, now that she knew Graham lived there, she could somehow feel his presence.

She worked through feeding the horses, even when her hands felt like they might fall off and they were bright red. By the time she checked all the cattle feeding troughs and took care of the ice, the salt licks, and the thrush that had popped up on a few of her cows, the daylight had begun to fade.

Every bone in Laney's body wanted to go back to the house and snuggle into a blanket with Bailey, hot chocolate warming her from the inside out as a movie played at low volume in front of them.

She found Bailey in the barn, cuddled up with the two dogs and the tablet Laney let her use after she did her chores. "Come on, Bay. I'm finally done."

The girl looked up at her and slowly got to her feet. "Did you know that orangutans' arms stretch out longer than their bodies?" She held her arms out as if she were an airplane. "Humans don't do that."

"I didn't know that," Laney said, smiling at the ground as they picked their way back to the homestead. Once inside, she slipped a pizza in the oven and changed out of her cold and wet clothes.

"Hot chocolate?" she asked her daughter, who had also changed and was now feeding the indoor dogs.

"Yeah, sure." Bailey wandered over to the couch and sat down while Laney zipped around the kitchen to get the mugs, milk, and powder out. With the first mug rotating in the microwave, she remembered Graham and his request to come help with his horses.

A groan pulled through her throat. She could easily text him and say she couldn't come. But part of her wanted to help him. The part that found it funny that he thought he could just show up in backcountry Wyoming and run a lodge and stables when he hadn't come back to Coral Canyon for much more than holiday dinners over the past two decades.

In the end, she finished the hot chocolate and pulled the pizza out of the oven when the timer went off. Bailey had switched on the TV, and Laney swept a kiss across her daughter's forehead. "I have to go help someone for a few minutes," she said. "Will you be okay here?"

Bailey took a sip of her hot chocolate while guilt pulled strongly through Laney. Although Bailey was only six years old, she could be alone for a half an hour.

"I'll lock the doors, and you've got Clearwater and Barry here," she said. "And the phone Grandma gave you. Call me if you need me. I'll just be up the road a bit."

Bailey nodded and went back to watching TV. Laney pulled her boots back on though her feet protested at the indication that they'd be returning to work.

It's for Graham Whittaker, she thought, hoping her old feet would get the message and just get the job done.

ALMOST ONE YEAR LATER

G raham woke before dawn, as usual. He lay in bed for a few minutes, because those moments were likely all he'd get in the way of peace and quiet that day. Most days, actually. Running Springside Energy was a seven-day-a-week job that he tried to cram into six so he could attend church.

Running Whiskey Mountain Lodge was easily as busy, what with the horses and the land and everything. So he'd hired three women on as staff around the lodge. Annie only came to clean a few times a week, because seventy percent of the house was still unused. Bree had seen to his lawn, gardens, pool, and trees over the summer and into the fall. Now that winter was breathing down their necks again, she'd asked about doing some interior decorating on the house.

Graham had looked around the foyer, finally noticing that while everything was dust-free thanks to Annie's efforts, there wasn't anything personal in the room. No pictures. No flower arrangements. No personal items of his travels, his likes, nothing.

Every room in the house felt like that, like it had no personality. Like the ghost of a man lived here.

Graham had nodded, which had brought a bright smile to Bree's face. So, for the past three weeks, she'd been bringing in holiday décor. For Thanksgiving, the whole place had been ripe with turkeys, welcome signs, a fall leaf wreath, and much more.

She'd just asked him about art, what he liked, what her budget was, and if each room should have a theme. He'd given her whatever money she needed and asked her to simply make the house look like someone cared about it.

Graham did care about the lodge; he really did. He lived in a large bedroom down the hall from the kitchen, with a huge office between the two. Those three rooms felt lived-in at least, and they took up almost the entire main floor. He used the washroom, where Bear slept, but it had been a while since he'd been up the spiral staircase to the rooms up there, or down to the basement, where more rooms, a game room, and a theater sat.

He swung his legs over the side of the bed and stretched, the scent of baking bread meeting his nose. His last addition to Whiskey Mountain Lodge had obviously arrived and had been busy in the kitchen.

Celia Armstrong was brilliant with flavors, and she could make anything Graham requested. He didn't make a lot of demands on her, other than "something I can't get from a place in town."

After all, Coral Canyon was a small place, and he'd eaten through every restaurant twice before May had arrived. That was when he hired Celia, then Bree, and finally Annie as the workload at Springside threatened to crush him.

He took a moment to miss his life in Seattle. He'd lived there for fourteen years and hadn't eaten at all the restaurants he'd wanted to, let alone every one in the city. After being gone for eleven months, he could think about that life without anger.

Thank you for that, he prayed, glad that time did seem to heal some wounds. He could even think about Erica and all she'd done without his pulse pounding in his neck, and that had taken much longer to achieve.

He ran his hands through his hair and got up to shower. After all, he had chores to do out in the stables before he got to work on energy business. Over the months, he'd learned a lot about horses, farming, and ranching.

Whenever there was something he didn't know, he called Laney. She'd come to help him, sometimes bringing her daughter and sometimes coming alone. And in a world where Graham had given up his corporate job, his friends, and his entire life, it was nice to have someone come when he called.

In fact, Laney McAllister was definitely one of his only friends in Wyoming. His brother and mother lived in town, but Graham honestly found it hard to get down to see them more than once a month.

He enjoyed being busy, because it prevented him from

having too much time to think, like he was now. So he put his lonely existence from his mind and got ready for the day.

When he arrived in the kitchen, he grinned at the spread of hot bread and homemade strawberry jam. "Celia." He chuckled as she turned from the stove. "You're a godsend."

She smiled at him, the wrinkles around her eyes a welcome sight. Her laughter like a balm to his weary soul. The older woman reminded him so much of his mother, and hiring her was the best move he'd made since coming to Coral Canyon.

"It's just bread, Graham."

"And eggs." He pointed to the pan behind her. She turned back to her scrambling, and Graham sliced the end off a loaf of bread and smeared it with butter and jam. A moan leaked from his throat at the warmth, the yeasty taste of the bread, the sugary jam.

"A godsend," he repeated around the mouthful of food, and Celia shook her head. A few moments later, she slid the eggs from the pan to a plate and presented them to him.

"I'm making those sweet and sour meatballs you love," she said. "So they'll last until I come back. And I've put three of those rising crust pizzas you love in the freezer. And Bree's coming to do the Christmas decorations this weekend, and since I'm visiting my sister." She lifted her eyebrows as if to ask if Graham remembered that she'd be gone.

He hadn't remembered, but he nodded anyway.

"Since I'll be visiting my sister, Bree's agreed to bring up the next batch of food."

"I can go to town," Graham said. "I think I can stand to go back to Towers again."

Celia laughed and swatted his arm. "You'll do no such thing. No one should eat a dozen onion rings the size of their head."

Graham smiled, took a couple bites of scrambled eggs just to appease her, and said, "I have to get out to the stable. Thanks for breakfast, Celia."

She grinned at him like he was her son, and said, "You work too hard."

"When there's work to be done," he said, his standard answer. And there was always work to be done. He stepped outside, the temperature about ten degrees colder than the day before. Now that December had arrived, Graham had been warned to expect snow every day until Christmas.

The scent of snow hung in the air, the tops of the Tetons already dusted with the white stuff. Gray clouds loitered ominously, and Graham stuffed his hat lower on his head and bent into the wind on the way down to the stable.

Frost covered everything, and the sight of it made anger slip through Graham's bloodstream. But he'd chosen this, and he couldn't be mad about it. Not anymore.

He still had the three horses that had come with the lodge—Bolt, Clover, and Goldie. Out of the three of them, he liked the gelding the best, and Bolt was the first to greet him, as usual. The other two horses were slowly warming up to him, and Graham had read that horses could be very loyal animals. They'd obviously loved their previous owner, and no matter how many apples he brought out to them, Clover and Goldie still gave him disdainful looks before coming over to eat.

At least he'd kept them all alive for almost a year. That right there was a major life accomplishment Graham had never aspired to. His phone rang, and Sam Buttars's name popped up on the screen.

His only other friend, and a grin tugged at the corners of Graham's mouth. "Hey, Sam," he said after opening the call.

"Graham, how are you?"

"Doin' fine," he said, feeling very cowboy-ish. He'd met up with Sam after discovering they had a mutual friend in Tucker Jenkins. Tucker actually bought the horse farm in Vermont where Sam and his brothers had worked for a few years. Ben, the youngest, was still there, but the other three brothers had moved on.

Sam lived on his father's farm with his wife Bonnie and their two kids. They'd had Graham over a few times over the past year, and he'd always enjoyed himself.

"Bonnie wanted you to come to dinner this weekend. Doable?"

Graham didn't have his schedule in front of him, but it didn't matter. He could spend eighty hours a week CEO-ing, and another twenty with the horses and buildings. Now the weather was turning bad, there wouldn't be nearly as much to do around the ranch besides keeping the horses alive.

"Definitely," he said. Bonnie was an excellent cook, and

his mouth started watering at the thought of her bacon and potato soup.

"Want to bring someone?" Sam asked, his voice a bit too high.

"What?" The word exploded out of Graham's mouth.

"Bonnie made me ask," Sam hissed into the phone. "She says it's not good for you to be holed up in that lodge all by yourself all the time."

"I'm not by myself," he said, reaching for the pitchfork. "Celia's here twice a week. Annie too. And Bree's coming this weekend to get the place ready for the holidays." And his entire family had committed to coming to Whiskey Mountain for Christmas as well. Though it was still three weeks off, a giddiness pranced through Graham's chest at the thought of having all of his brothers and his mom together for a few days.

They hadn't been able to gather that last Christmas, and his dad had died only five days later. So when he'd offered the lodge this year, everyone had said yes, and Graham had already talked to Annie, Celia, and Bree about helping him get everything ready for the celebration.

Sam sighed. "I know," he said. "Bonnie worries about you."

"Tell Bonnie I'm just fine."

"Bring someone if you want!" Her voice came through the line as though she was standing in the kitchen Sam had remodeled for her while he sat at the table. Sam chuckled, but Graham didn't.

He didn't need to be thinking about dating. Not right now. He had no time to give to someone, number one. And number two, he'd left most of his heart in Seattle. How was it fair to give a slice of himself to someone and expect it to be enough?

"Tomorrow night," Sam said. "Six o'clock."

Graham confirmed, hung up, and shook his head. "They want me to bring someone," he said to Bolt with a scoff. "That's ridiculous, right?"

The horse didn't answer, but lifted his head over the fence and nudged Graham's shoulder. At first, the large animals had scared him a little. But now he found them gentle and attentive.

"You're lucky," he said to Bolt. "You've got two ladies right here, penned in with you so they can't escape." He rubbed one palm down the horse's mane. "And you always know where they are, so they can't cheat on you."

His throat cinched, and he swallowed back the bitter memories. He wasn't even sure he could trust another woman, and he thought he was doing just fine as a cowboy bachelor.

Wasn't he?

———

THE FOLLOWING EVENING, HE SHOWED UP AT SAM'S farmhouse ten minutes early. It was a Saturday after all, and he couldn't be expected to work twelve hours on the weekend. But he had, and still had time to shower and drive down the winding roads from the lodge to the town.

Sam and Bonnie lived on the east side, and Graham enjoyed a trip down memory lane as he drove from one side of the town to the other. Sam and his brothers had grown up here too, but Sam sat between Eli and Beau, Graham's two youngest brothers. Graham had been gone from Coral Canyon before Sam entered high school.

Bonnie opened the front door and waved at him to come on in. Graham ducked his head and got out of the huge, hulking SUV he drove. "Hey, Bonnie," he called.

"Use the side door." She hurried to close the door, and Graham didn't blame her. It was freezing tonight, and he couldn't see a single star as he walked toward the stairs leading to the entrance on the side of the house.

So it would definitely snow tonight, and Graham felt a little piece of him die. He never thought he'd miss Seattle and all the rain, but snow was definitely worse.

Inside the house, the atmosphere held cheer, bright yellow light, and the scent of roasted meat mixed with baby powder.

Sam had a child in each arm. His daughter, Jackie, had just turned three, and she squealed when she saw Graham. He took her from Sam and produced the bag of chocolate that made him so popular with the little girl.

"There are only fifteen of them," he said to Bonnie when she tsk'ed. Jackie already had the first candy-coated chocolate in her hand, a blue one.

"Blue," she said before popping it into her mouth.

Graham smiled at her and set her on her feet.

"Not in the living room, Jackie," Bonnie said as she stirred something on the stove. "Eat them at the table."

Sam smiled and shook Graham's hand, the six-month-old baby boy on his hip bouncing with the movement. CJ babbled and slobbered on his fingers, and Graham gave him a cursory smile. He'd never thought of himself as cut out for fatherhood, so seeing Sam in the role so easily was a bit of a mystery to him.

"Something smells good," he said to Bonnie as he removed his cowboy hat and set it out of the way on the back counter.

"Beef tacos," she said. "We bought a cow from your neighbor."

"Laney?"

"Yes, Laney." Bonnie turned off the stove and declared them ready to eat. A flurry of activity started then, from saying grace to loading up plates for small hands. By the time everyone sat at the table with flour tortillas, long strips of marinated beef, and all the taco toppings, several minutes had passed.

Yet Bonnie said, "She's single, you know," as if no time had passed.

"Who?" Graham asked.

"Laney." Bonnie rolled her eyes. "About your age too."

Graham took a big bite of his taco, not sure where Bonnie was going with the conversation. He exchanged a glance with Sam, who was absolutely no help.

"I know Laney," Graham said after he swallowed. "We grew up together. We're good friends."

Bonnie's eyebrows went up. "You mean you have other friends besides us?" Her hazel eyes danced with merriment.

Graham smiled and shook his head. "I've needed help

with the stable chores from time to time. Laney comes when I call her."

"Like a servant?" Bonnie's hand paused with a taco halfway to her mouth.

"No," he said quickly, though Laney did come whenever he called. Maybe not right away, but she always had. Sometimes she looked absolutely exhausted, but she was still there. He had the sudden thought to invite her for Christmas. Her and her mother, who still lived in town. But he kept the idea to himself, sure Bonnie would have them engaged and their wedding planned if he said anything at all.

"Well, she's beautiful," Bonnie said. "And she hasn't gone out with anyone in years." She was less than subtle with the hints, and Graham nodded and smiled like he agreed that he'd go straight home and ask Laney to dinner.

Sam, thankfully, moved the topic to something else, but Graham couldn't let go of the idea of not only asking Laney to come to the lodge for Christmas but to go out with him.

CHAPTER 3

L aney wasn't sure she could make it through another winter alone. Last year had almost killed her, and the snow hadn't melted until well into May.

I need help, she prayed. *And someone cheap.* The ranch made enough to function, plus a little bit more. Barely enough to keep her and Bailey in new clothes, keep the homestead heated, and put gas in the truck and other ranch vehicles.

I don't want to sell a horse, she continued her prayer. *Please, help me find a solution to this problem.*

The work around the ranch in the snow slowed her down, and she didn't have time to lose. But she knew she couldn't keep going at the rate she was. She'd turned forty last March, and her body was starting to make her feel it every day of her life.

Still, she bundled up and left Bailey on the couch with the heelers to go out and get the morning feeding done.

Graham's invitation to Christmas at the lodge sat on her voicemail, and she dialed it just to hear his voice again. True, the man had annoyed her these last eleven months, always calling and demanding she come help him with some problem on his property.

Or maybe she'd just viewed his requests as demands. A time or two, he'd acted completely beastly when she'd shown up, but she'd helped him, vowed to ignore him next time, and then responded to his calls anyway.

The cycle made no sense. Neither did her perpetual attraction to him. She reasoned that anyone with two X-chromosomes would be attracted to Graham Whittaker. In fact, she'd heard his name tossed around the rumor mill in town more than once.

But, to her knowledge, he'd never been out with anyone. Hardly ever left the lodge, in fact. He'd hired a staff to help him, and while Springside Energy sometimes found itself in the headlines, he'd kept them off the Internet's front page for almost a year.

"Hey, Laney," her voicemail recited back to her. "It's Graham." A chuckle, which sounded kind of nervous. "Of course it's Graham. Your phone will tell you that." He cleared his throat, another tell of anxiety. "I'm just wondering what your holiday plans are. My brothers are all coming to town, and we're having a big celebration at the lodge. Would love to have you and Bailey there with us. Your mother too."

Her heart warmed every time she listened to the message, and she wouldn't allow herself to admit how often that was.

"Let me know." The message ended, and Laney ended the call to voicemail, tucked the phone in her back pocket, and got to work. She hadn't answered Graham yet, and it had been almost a week. Would he still have her? Wouldn't he need to plan food, activities?

"Probably not," she said to Acorn, the horse in the first stall. "He has people bring his groceries and cook his meals. What's two more? Or three?" she added, thinking of her mother. They hadn't discussed any plans for Christmas, though Laney knew she could show up at her mom's unannounced and an hour later, there would be a feast on the table.

She went down the west wall of the stable, feeding the horses, checking their blankets to make sure they fit properly and didn't have sores, and cleaning any stalls that hadn't been done recently.

At the end of the row, she pulled out her phone and called her mom.

"Laney." Her mother always infused a measure of surprise into her voice when she answered the phone.

"Hey, Mom." Laney took a moment to lean against the wall, giving some relief to her legs. Her wrist ached from the sprain she'd gotten over the summer, trying to lift a hay bale that was simply too heavy for her. "I'm wondering what you want to do for Christmas. Graham Whittaker has invited us to come to the lodge and spend it with his family."

"Oh, that sounds lovely," her mom said. She sounded tired, and the fact that she'd agreed so readily testified of it.

"I'll tell him yes, then?" She wasn't sure why she'd made the statement a question, only that she needed extra support to accept the invitation.

"I think it sounds nice to just be guests for a year," her mother said. "Don't you?"

The thought of not having to decorate, cook, clean, anything did sound like heaven. Maybe it was a heavenly intervention. Maybe the help she'd been praying for. And she wasn't one to tell the Lord how He should do things.

"All right," she said. "I'll let him know we'll be there." After a few more pleasantries, Laney hung up and drew her shoulders up straight. She had a phone call to make, and it wasn't going to be easy.

———

THE WEATHER WORSENED AS THE DAYS PASSED, AND WITH only a week until Christmas a healthy three feet of snow sat on the ground at the ranch. No other solution to Laney's problems presented itself, and she carried on each day the best she could.

That was all God could ask of her, wasn't it? *Just do your best.*

Pastor Landy hadn't said exactly that, but that was the message she'd taken from his last sermon. She had seen Graham at church occasionally, but he never acknowledged her or sat by her.

She wasn't sure why the slight bothered her. Only that it did.

The party at the lodge was in only three days, and she

was looking forward to seeing the interior now that it had been remodeled. She wasn't sure if he knew that a fire had destroyed most of the main floor and half the rooms on the second level, but she knew. The construction vehicles in and out of that place had disturbed her favorite horse, Starlight, for months while they renovated it.

When she stepped out of the shower, the hot spray had not done much for the ache in her shoulder. "Definitely going to snow today." She moaned as she rotated her arm, trying to further loosen the stiffness there.

The more she worked, the harder it snowed, until it finally drove her back into the house about mid-afternoon. The sky was as dark as though it was night, and she shook the heavy flakes from her hat and coat before ducking into the house.

"Phew." She blew her breath out, glad the heat in the homestead still worked so well. She'd been told years ago that the furnace would need to be replaced in the next three to five years, but it had been almost eight now, and the appliance was still kicking.

A blessing, she thought as she called, "Bay? Where are you?" The little girl had finished school for the holidays two days before and usually had no problem entertaining herself. She spent most of her free time on the couch with the dogs, a movie on, or music playing while she colored.

But as Laney bent to untie her boots, she couldn't see any living thing, canine or human. Still no answer. Laney hurried through the rest of her undressing, finally getting all the heavy, sopping clothes off. She'd normally hang them all to dry but she left them in a heap as she went to search for Bailey.

She found her daughter asleep on the bed, both dogs curled around her, one on each side. Clearwater, the oldest of the blue heelers, looked up with a sleepy expression on his face. Barry just glanced at her without moving his head, making his face look baleful, like *we had to jump onto the bed. The girl human was in here and we didn't want her to be alone.*

"Come on." She snapped her fingers and both dogs came over to her. Bailey didn't move, and Laney decided to let her sleep. With the dogs out in the hall, she gently closed the door and went to find something to put in the oven for dinner.

With a sheet pan of corndogs and frozen French fries in a piping hot oven, she'd collapsed onto the couch and taken two breaths when the power went out.

"No," she groaned and heaved herself back off the couch. This couldn't be happening. Without electricity, they couldn't heat the house. And it would get awfully cold in here, as she hadn't had the money to replace the drafty windows as she'd been advised.

She checked the breaker box in the basement, but all the connections seemed fine. Her stomach grumbled for want of food, and Laney remembered that she'd skipped lunch in an effort to get the ranch chores done amidst the swirling storm.

And now that wind and snow had knocked out her power.

She hurried back upstairs, because it was way too cold

in the basement already. Pulling on a coat, she opened Bailey's door. She hated to wake the girl, but they couldn't stay here. If they could get to town, they could sleep at her mother's and come do the minimal feeding chores when they could.

"Bailey." She nudged the angelic child and her daughter's eyes fluttered open. "Sweetheart, the power's out, and we have to go." The light was gray, but Laney could see enough to pack a bag with the essentials for a couple of nights at her mother's. With a backpack on Bailey's shoulders with her pajamas and clothes in it, and a bag in her hand, Laney started collecting the boots, hats, coats, scarves, and gloves they needed. She'd lived on the ranch long enough to know a couple of things. One, in a storm, always overfeed. She'd done that today, so her animals would be all right if she couldn't make it out tomorrow. Two, never leave the house without as much gear as possible.

Even though they'd be in the car, she wasn't going to take any chances. There were plenty of opportunities to slide off the road, and the snowplows wouldn't make it out this far for days. Her ranch and the lodge were the only sources of shelter.

Worry ate at her stomach, and she wondered if they'd even be able to get to town. "Come on," she said to Bailey and the dogs in a falsely cheery voice. "Get in the truck." She hit the auto-opener on the garage and stared as it sat there.

Of course. There was no power. She got out and bent to lift the door with her hands.

At least three feet of snow had fallen that day. How had she not noticed? Probably because she kept her head down as she worked, the wind so violent it whipped the snow into her eyes if she didn't.

Bailey got in the truck like the sun shone and they were going to the beach while both dogs jumped in the back, ready for the adventure. Laney couldn't get herself to move. She wasn't even sure she could get out of her own driveway.

Can't stay here, she thought. *Can't get out.*

Desperation clawed at her now, scattering her thoughts. In moments like these, she hated being the only one capable of making a decision. She needed *help.* A partner to talk to, to bounce ideas off of, to rely on when she simply had nothing left to give. And Laney was operating on empty right now, and had been for weeks.

"Can't stay here," she muttered to herself, though she wondered if bundling up in a single room was the lesser of two evils. She honestly had no idea what she should do, but she knew she couldn't stay here.

She returned to the truck, where the heater blew. Her phone rang before she could put the vehicle in reverse.

"Graham," she breathed into the phone, relief soaring through her. He'd help. He drove a massive SUV that drank gas like it was free. He'd come get them.

"Where are you?" he asked. "Inside, I hope."

"I'm standing in my garage," she said. "My power's out."

"It is? It's on here."

"We probably have different lines." And his were

newer, thanks to the fire from two years ago. Everything had been replaced.

"Can you get out?"

She eyed the snow and then the clearance on her truck. "I honestly don't know. Bailey's in the truck, but I'm not sure leaving is the best idea."

"You can't stay there without heat. Do you have a fireplace?"

"No," she said. "Well, I do, but it's in the basement, and I've closed it off since we never go down there." She moved to the edge of the garage, where snow met cement.

He exhaled. "I'll come get you. You can stay here tonight."

"Oh, that's not necessary. I—"

"You can't make it to town," he said. "I can guarantee that." He spoke in that voice she hated, the one that bossed people around and expected to be obeyed.

"How do you know?" she challenged.

"Because my housekeeper just tried to leave in her four-wheel-drive truck, and she slid off the road a quarter of a mile down. She's staying here tonight too."

Maybe longer, Laney thought. The sky foamed with snow, and all she could see was gray in every direction as the snow flurried through it.

"And you think you can get down here and back to your place?"

"I'll have to try." Scuffling came through his end of the line, and he said, "I'm on my way. Hold tight."

The call ended, and Laney had no other choice but to do what he said, as much as that irked her. She'd spent three years doing what Mike had suggested, and that hadn't ended well for her.

He'd never once said he didn't want to live on the ranch. He'd known from day one that she'd inherit Echo Ridge one day, that she wanted to spend her life working the land and raising cattle. He'd claimed to be on the same page as her.

He'd only lasted nine months on the ranch before he'd left.

She pushed the thoughts away and stepped over to the passenger door. "Come on out, Bay. Graham's going to come pick us up." She stood at the mouth of the garage with one hand clutching her bag and the other placed protectively on Bailey's shoulder, the snow swirling, swirling, swirling down.

CHAPTER 4

Graham fought the steering wheel, praying out loud that he could make it the mile to Laney's house to get her and Bailey.

"Please," he said again. "Come on. They can't stay there. Help us out a little. No." He jerked the wheel to the right as the Hummer started to slide, and it corrected. He stomped on the accelerator and added, "Please, Lord. She needs help," while the wheels spun.

They finally caught and he shot forward, his fingers so tight around the wheel they ached. And he'd only gone about two hundred yards. Or so he thought. He wasn't really sure. After all, he was the man who'd wandered onto someone else's property and didn't even know it. And in this storm, the landscape had no identifying features whatsoever.

He caught sight of a flashing red light, and he hit the brakes. The vehicle stopped easier than it had started, and he slowly pulled down what he hoped was the driveway. The red brake lights guided him until he could make out the blackness of the garage among the wall of gray, and with it, a small figure standing on the edge of the snow.

He parked and jumped out. "Hey," he called. The brake lights went off and Laney climbed from the truck. "Smart about the lights."

"I wasn't sure you'd be able to find me," she said, bending to pick up her bag. "I hope you have room for us and two dogs." Her eyes held truckloads of worry, and Graham wanted to erase it for her.

"Of course," he said. "Let's get them in." He held up one hand. "I'll do it. You wait." He approached Bailey first. "You ready, small pint?"

She smiled up at him. "Ready."

"I'm going to pick you up. Hold onto me, okay?" He swept the child into his arms and hurried through the snow to the passenger side of the vehicle. He put her inside and slammed the door before retracing his steps. "Dogs next." He grabbed one and repeated the high-step through the snow to the Hummer.

Once both dogs were in, he stood in the garage with Laney and clapped his cold hand together. "You want me to carry you?"

She snorted. "I can step in your footprints." She gripped her bag tighter like she might swing it at him if he even touched her. He thought of that single moment outside her cabin, almost a year ago, when he'd held her hand. She wore the same wariness in her expression now as she had then, and Graham gestured for her to go first.

"After you."

She danced through his footprints and got in the Hummer, adjusting her bag on her lap before pulling the door closed. He turned to close the garage door, and when he entered her house, it had already grown colder though her power surely hadn't gone out too long ago.

He wanted to stay in this space that belonged to Laney, but he forced himself to turn toward the front door and leave, locking it behind him. Then he dashed back to the driver's seat and said, "Let's pray we can get back to the lodge."

He made his prayers silent, but Bailey in the backseat started saying, "Lord, help us get back to the lodge," in the sweetest, high-pitched voice Graham had ever heard. In a normal situation, he might've exchanged a glance with Laney, but he didn't trust himself not to drive them right off the road.

"Amen," he whispered, his fingers tightening around the wheel as he backed out of the driveway and aimed the truck toward the hill leading up to the lodge. How had he never noticed that this hill was like climbing Mount Everest?

Probably because he always called Laney to his place and very rarely went to hers. Fine, he'd never been down to her ranch, besides that one trespassing incident almost a year ago. But he was very aware of her sitting next to him in the Hummer, the scent of her skin and her fear heavy in the air between them.

His heart pounded at triple-time, one a normal heartbeat. One with anxiety over getting up the hill, and one because he'd been thinking about Laney as more than his best friend for a few weeks now and he had no idea how to handle those feelings.

Or if he even had feelings. Maybe Bonnie had just poisoned his mind, and now all he could do when it came to Laney was think about taking her to dinner.

The tires slipped, and Graham pressed the four-wheel-drive button. They caught again, propelling them up the hill. With the accelerator pressed all the way to the floor, he managed to shoot the vehicle and all its occupants toward the lodge.

Having tracks to guide him helped, but it still felt like he was trying to push an entire mountain's worth of snow with just two tires.

The lights in the lodge glinted in the darkness, and he thought that no matter what, they could walk there now. Relief spread through him slowly—not enough to get him to ease up on his grip or the gas. He finally did, though, so he wouldn't drive them right off the edge of the hill.

Coming from town, the entrance to his place was straight. Coming from Laney's, he had to make a right turn and go down a long driveway and past a small parking lot. The turn proved to be the hardest, and the back wheels fishtailed a little.

He pumped the gas and jerked the wheel, and the expensive vehicle righted itself. Thirty seconds later, he pulled to a stop underneath the rooftop that went over the circle drive. The wind had blown in some snow, but it wasn't three feet worth. The wipers continued at double-time, and as he peeled his stiff fingers from the steering wheel, his heart calmed slightly. "We made it."

He'd been shoveling the front steps all day, so he didn't have to carry anyone, and a few seconds later, they burst into the warm and cozy lodge. Bree had done a fantastic job of making the lodge look like someone lived there and cared about each room, each piece of tile, each decoration.

"Wow."

Graham glanced at Bailey and found her soaking in the foyer, where a wreath ten feet across had been hung from the banister on the second floor. Nativities dotted the shelves and counter tops, and pine boughs and poinsettias laced their way through the spiral stair railing as it went up.

"This is beautiful," Laney agreed, her eyes also darting around and drinking everything in.

"We're doing a tree lighting in a few days," he said. "I think I told you about it." He stepped forward, trying to ignore the things he hadn't picked out but would have to take credit for. He wasn't sure why the idea bothered him so much. "You never said if you'd come or not." He flashed Laney a tight smile and indicated the stairs. "I'll help you get settled upstairs. Annie's up there too, and there's plenty of space, bathrooms, all of that."

He went first, because Laney and Bailey didn't move. His action must've prompted theirs, because he heard Laney murmur something to her daughter and then their footsteps followed his.

He hated giving tours of the lodge, but he'd been gearing himself up to do exactly that. In three more days, his entire family would be here, and he'd have to play the perfect host with the perfect party. He didn't mind that part—heck, he was actually good at hosting parties. But he was not good at concealing his emotions or pretending like he cared about wreaths, ornaments, or Christmas trees.

He wasn't a Scrooge. He just had more on his plate than bells, gingerbread men, and sleigh rides.

"So she's in here." He pointed to the door at the top of the stairs. "But there are five other bedrooms up here." Graham paused. A bedroom was a bedroom. "You can take your pick."

"Can I choose, Mom?" Bailey's face had some color in it now, and she danced ahead of her mom.

Laney chuckled and said, "Yeah, go pick one." The little girl ran off, and Graham caught the adoration in her mother's eyes. She switched her gaze to his, and the feeling faded. She looked at him with...appreciation? Hesitancy? Longing?

Graham wasn't sure. Her blue heelers came up the steps and sat by her, and she absently stroked one of their heads. "Thank you, Graham," she said. "For letting us stay here. I'm sure we'll be out of your hair in the morning."

He was sure she wouldn't be—and he didn't mind. In fact, he hoped she'd have to stay so he could maybe get to feel what it would be like to have her fingers rake through his hair....

He blinked, unsure of where such a thought had come from. This was Laney. His best friend here in Wyoming. The woman who'd helped him figure out how to take care of horses, and his water rights, and a million other tiny little things he didn't know about barns, stables, and animals.

Was he her best friend too?

Surely not. She'd lived here a lot longer than him, and he thought there wasn't anything the woman couldn't do.

"Stay as long as you like," he said, his voice rough around the edges. He cleared his throat. "Celia left a pot roast in the slow cooker last night, so that's what we're eatin' tonight too. Should be ready any time you're hungry." He walked toward the stairs before he said something he couldn't take back.

"Graham—" Laney started, but Bailey squealed and said, "Mom! Come see this tub!" and her attention switched to her daughter.

Didn't matter. She'd already said thanks, and that was all Graham needed. Honestly, he didn't even need that. He had the house, the amenities, the electricity, and the money to have dozens of people live with him. He could handle two more, even if Laney did have the most beautiful eyes he'd ever seen.

———

GRAHAM PACED IN HIS OFFICE, FEELING LIKE A CAGED TIGER. This snow didn't do anyone any good, and he wondered if God could somehow get a memo to Mother Nature to stop already.

But the snow kept drifting down as furiously as ever. At this rate, his family would be lucky to be able to fly in, let alone make the hour-long drive to Coral Canyon from the airport.

He couldn't believe he'd categorized Laney's eyes as beautiful. He'd always thought so though, even in high school and before that, when they'd become friends as kids. Her kindness shone in those light green depths, and he turned from the window where he'd been watching the snow.

"She's your neighbor," he told himself, not for the first time. "She has a daughter."

Just because Bonnie had suggested her as a possible date didn't mean she was interested in him. He hadn't given her much of a reason to be, what with calling her all the time and demanding her help.

He remembered how tired she looked, and he hoped she'd be able to recharge and relax here at the lodge. When he'd first bought the place, that calming atmosphere had been what called to him the most. The lodge spoke of a place to come when a person was weary, and he'd bought it with cash on the spot.

His phone chimed out the reminder he'd set: *time for dinner*.

The afternoon had gotten away from him, what with all the commotion and rescuing. So he silenced the alarm and left the office in favor of the kitchen, which sat just down the hall on the left. The scent of roasted meat met his nose, and his mouth watered the tiniest bit.

Annie stood at the counter, using a pair of tongs to toss a huge bowl of green salad. "The potatoes are almost done."

Graham knew how to open an oven, but he could see the timer on the front, and it said five minutes. "Okay." He glanced around, trying to remember where Celia got the plates from.

Annie, who seemed to be able to sense his thoughts, pointed to the cupboard next to the stove. "Plates in there, if you want to get them down. I'll get out the silverware." She set the tongs in the bowl and opened a drawer.

Graham got down four plates, which was four times as many as normal. In fact, even eating on a plate was more than he usually did. Though he'd never tell Celia he ate her food right out of the pot she left it in, that was exactly what he did most nights.

And salad? He eyed the vegetables like they might sprout to life and attack him. They didn't, and he turned back to the oven when the timer went off. Proud of himself for knowing where the oven mitts were, he retrieved them from the hook on the side of the cupboard and pulled out the baked potatoes. He then opened the fridge and got out sour cream, cheddar cheese, ranch dressing, and a container of bacon bits.

Annie arranged everything and looked at him. "So. We're ready. Should we wait?"

"I didn't tell them specifically what time dinner was," he said, glancing up like he could see through the ceiling and into whichever bedroom Laney and Bailey had chosen. "I'll text her." He wasn't sure he trusted himself to be alone with Laney and not say or do something that would put their friendship in jeopardy.

After all, wasn't that exactly what Erica had told him?

You work too much. It's your own fault I had to find someone else to be with.

As if her cheating was his fault. And if those words hadn't been sharp enough, she'd also said *We were better off as friends.*

He'd texted her a lot for help too, as she was the administrative assistant in his department and he often needed her to do things for him.

Shaking the past from his mind, he texted Laney. *Dinner's ready. Come down now if you want to eat with me and Annie.*

She didn't answer right away, and Graham pocketed his phone as his stomach growled. Shoveling snow and tromping through snow and driving through snow really worked up his appetite.

"Let's eat," he said to Annie. "They can eat whenever they come down."

CHAPTER 5

Laney glanced at Bailey, who slumbered on the
bottom bunk in the bedroom she'd chosen. She'd
taken a bath in the big, free-standing, clawfoot tub and
then fallen asleep with her silky hair still twisted in the
towel on her head.

Laney felt as weary as Bailey, especially after her own
hot shower. She'd put on a pair of yoga pants and a T-shirt,
and had been running a brush through her hair when
Graham had texted.

*Dinner's ready. Come down now if you want to eat with me
and Annie.*

"Come down now," she repeated, shaking her head. He
really was the beast from that children's fairy tale. *If she
doesn't eat with me, she doesn't eat at all* ran through her
head, and she set her phone on the dresser so she wouldn't
answer him immediately.

She didn't want to wake her daughter, but she was

hungry. Graham could wait a few minutes to get a reply, and Laney wouldn't wither away if she didn't eat for another little bit. She moved to the window and watched the weather outside.

The visibility couldn't be more than five feet, as she couldn't see even the tall trees she knew stood in the back yard. Clearwater whined, and Laney automatically bent down to scratch the dog's head.

"I know," she said, though she had no idea what she knew. She knew she'd been fighting feelings for Graham Whittaker since her teen years. Sure, she'd gotten over him pretty fast when he'd left Coral Canyon and gone to college. Then she'd met Mike and fallen madly in love. They'd only been together for four years and had been divorced for three.

No, she hadn't thought about Graham during her marriage. Or at all in the years since Mike had left. Well, until this past year, with Graham back in her life—sort of—and Mike out of it.

Her ridiculous feelings had been what kept her heading over to his place whenever he texted or called. Her insane hope had ballooned with each interaction, and she hated that she always crashed after their brief encounters.

Sometimes he didn't even *look* at her when she came to help him. To be fair, he was shouldering the huge burden of running the energy company, as well as trying to learn how to manage horses, the lodge, and the land that came with it.

But he was wealthy, and he hadn't had to do all the

work required. If she could afford a housekeeper and a cook, she'd have them too.

Barry barked, startling Laney away from the window. "Shh," she chastised the dog, casting a quick glance at Bailey, who hadn't moved or awakened. "What's wrong?"

A big, black lab poked his head around the corner, clearly the source of the barking from Barry. "Hey, there." She smiled at the dog, who had white hairs around his mouth and nose. He was clearly old, and nothing of a threat, as he came around the corner slowly, his tongue hanging out of his mouth and his eyes drifting halfway shut as if to say *Hey, guys. Want to take a nap together?*

Laney greeted him and crouched down to stroke his head and scrub behind his ears. "What's your name, huh?" She caught his tags and twisted them so she could read them. "Bear." She grinned at the dog. "Seems about right." She let him move on and sniff her dogs, and the three of them started a chain to get to all the best parts of each other.

She hadn't pegged Graham as a dog-lover, and she'd never seen the lab around the lodge. Did he keep the animal confined to the house? After all, Laney hadn't been inside the lodge for years—not since she and Mike had been married here—and she really liked that it looked nothing the same.

No, this Whiskey Mountain Lodge was fit for celebrity weddings and receptions—and not the country bumpkin kind she'd had. No wonder the previous owner had sold. This place was too ritzy for the clientele Coral Canyon normally attracted, and she knew Will had had trouble keeping the place filled.

Although Jackson Hole—an upscale, very touristy, artsy-fartsy hot spot in Wyoming—only sat about a half an hour down the highway, Coral Canyon enjoyed a slower pace of life. One Laney really liked and didn't want replaced with what Jackson had, especially if the people were going to be coming within a mile of her front door..

But Graham wasn't using the lodge for its intended purposes. Though the rooms didn't have an ounce of dust in them, they also had a general feel of disuse. Emptiness. Abandonment.

All the sheets were clean, and every room had beds that were made up. She wondered if Graham had seen to that or hired someone. If she was a betting woman, Laney had her money on the housekeeper.

Bailey moaned, and Laney decided that was a great time to wake her and go get something to eat. She couldn't stay asleep much longer anyway, or she wouldn't go to bed that night.

"Bay." Laney swept her fingers across her daughter's forehead, smiling when her blue eyes opened sleepily. "Are you hungry? Want to go eat something?"

"Yeah." Bailey yawned and Laney helped her up.

"Let's brush your hair out first." Laney turned to find Bailey's backpack and found all three dogs curled up together at the foot of the bed. She chuckled, pulled out Bailey's brush, and ran it through her daughter's hair. "All right. Let's go see what this cowboy bachelor eats."

They held hands on the way down, and Laney counted

eighteen steps from the second floor to the first. Every-thing about the lodge seemed super-sized, including the man who sat at the dining room table with a strawberry blonde at least a decade younger than him. Annie Pruitt. She cleaned a lot of places around town, as her family owned the only residential maid service in Coral Canyon.

"Hey." Laney passed in the lane between the dining room and the kitchen, glancing to her right where they ate, and then left, where a huge kitchen waited. She'd seriously never seen so many cupboards before. An island ran down the middle of it, and her heart squeezed with jealousy when she saw the double ovens.

"Beef roast." Graham touched her lower back, which made Laney jump. She hadn't even heard him get up. "Right there." He guided her over to the food as if she couldn't see the big, black pot of meat, the tray of foil-wrapped baked potatoes, and the bowl of salad the size of Rhode Island.

How many people was he expecting?

"Hey, Bailey," he said. "Want me to help you?" He glanced at Laney, but not nearly long enough to make true eye contact, and picked up a plate. The little girl tucked her hair shyly and looked at Laney.

"Go on."

Bailey was used to having Laney or her grandmother help her, but she fell easily into bossing Graham around, and demanding more croutons, and saying she didn't want ranch on her potato.

Laney kept her smile to herself as she made her loaded baked potato and took more beef roast than she probably should've. But she loved a good roast, and it had been far too long since she'd had one. She took a seat across from Graham, which was probably a bad move, since she'd have to look at that gorgeous face during dinner.

"Mm," she moaned as she took her first bite, with the au jus practically dripping down her chin. "Where did you get this?"

"It's one of yours," Annie said, flashing a smile in Laney's direction.

Pride flashed through Laney, but she shrugged one shoulder as if it didn't matter if the beef had come from her biggest rival. "Oh, well, it's delicious." She took another bite and watched Graham as he practically inhaled the food on his plate. He had very little salad and quite a lot of meat, and Laney supposed he needed the protein to keep all those muscles in such good shape.

Embarrassed by the course of her thoughts, she ducked her head and filled her mouth with more food. Graham wasn't particularly loquacious, but Laney wasn't either. So the scraping of silverware against china became the only sounds.

"Where are you living now?" Laney finally asked Annie.

"I'm on Blackberry." She took a long drink of her water. "I live with my sister." She flicked her eyes toward Graham. "She thinks I'm the luckiest woman on the planet."

"Why's that?" Laney watched Graham, and though he didn't look up or react, he was definitely listening to the conversation.

Annie cocked her head toward Graham. "You know."

Oh, Laney knew, but she wanted Annie to say it out loud. "She thinks Graham is…handsome?"

That brought his head up and his eyes to hers for the first time that evening. He did have exquisite eyes, and Laney had lost herself to them many times.

Annie twittered and nodded before collecting her plate and standing up. She moved into the kitchen, and still Laney and Graham stared at one another. Annie said something, but Laney didn't know what.

Graham seemed to have his faculties about him, because he nodded and said, "Sure, thanks, Annie," without removing his eyes from Laney's.

Heat started to fill her from top to bottom, making her skin sear.

"Mom?"

She finally tore her gaze from Graham's, feeling a bit light-headed and definitely like she'd just confessed her teenage crush on him, and the one she'd been entertaining since his return to Coral Canyon.

"Hmm? Yeah?"

"I was wondering if I could feed the dogs and play with them." Bailey looked at her, and Laney examined her daughter's plate.

"You didn't eat a whole lot."

"I'm not that hungry."

"The dogs can eat it," Graham said.

Laney automatically didn't want Bailey to feed the table scraps to the dogs, though they fed their blue heelers leftovers all the time. There was just something about how he said things like they were law and all would follow his directions, no matter what.

In the end, she nodded to Bailey, who took her plate into the kitchen and set it near the dog bowls on the far side of the room. Annie worked in the kitchen, putting away the leftover food, and they seemed far away from the bubble around Laney and Graham.

"Hey," he said, drawing her attention back to him. Something about him had softened, and Laney felt her whole body turning into a warm marshmallow. It had been such a long time that a man had made her feel this way, she had no defense and no way to keep herself from swooning over him.

"What are you going to do tonight?" he asked.

Her eyebrows went up. "I don't know." She rarely had any time to herself, and even when she did, there was work to be done around the house. Dishes. Laundry. Bills. Dogs. Bailey. If she was lucky, she got in twenty minutes of reading while she lay in bed. Most of the time, she fell asleep with the e-reader on her chest and woke sometime in the middle of the night when Barry started snoring.

"Maybe you'd like to watch a movie." He cut a glance toward the kitchen, but Annie kept her focus on the chores.

Surprise pulled through Laney. "I can't remember the last time I watched a movie." As soon as the words left her mouth, she wanted to suck them back in. "I mean—"

"I know exactly what you mean." His hand moved across the table and touched hers. Almost in the same instant, he pulled it back almost like he'd been shocked.

Laney certainly had been, physically and mentally. She blinked at him, willing him to explain himself.

Instead, he picked up his cowboy hat and stuffed it on his head. "We work too much." He stood, leaving his plate on the table like a servant would come around and clean up after him. In fact, that was exactly what Annie did, swooping in to take the dish and go back into the kitchen.

Graham had gone through the arched doorway that led into the foyer, but his bootsteps now moved down the hall to the south side of the house, fading until Laney couldn't hear them anymore.

What on earth had just happened?

———

We work too much. We work too much. We work too much.

The words reverberated around inside her head long after she'd helped Annie get all the food put away. She sat on a plush couch in a comfortable living room with Annie down on the other end while Bailey played with the dogs on the floor. Annie put something on the TV that was entertaining enough, not that Laney had been able to focus on it.

Oh, no. All she could think about was Graham, where he'd gone, and when he might return. Was he working?

"Does he work all the time?" she asked Annie, who swiveled her head toward Laney.

"What?"

"Graham. Does he work all the time?"

Annie shrugged. "Most of the time, yeah. He won't let me in that office of his, and whew." She waved her hand in front of her nose. "I wouldn't go in there even if he did."

Laney had the sudden urge to see Graham's office. She couldn't imagine it being anything but straight-laced and orderly, but Annie's assessment was clearly different.

A half an hour passed, and Laney was about to suggest bed to Bailey, when Graham appeared. "We could put something on in the theater room," he said, his voice much softer than any previous Laney had heard him use.

Annie switched off the TV with an exaggerated yawn. "Oh, I'm tired. I'm going to head to bed."

"Bailey needs to get to bed too." Laney met her daughter's eyes, already prepared for the fight. "It's already twenty minutes past your bedtime, and the dogs can sleep with you." She cocked her head in Graham's direction without looking at him. "Well, our dogs can. I don't know about Bear."

"If he can get on the bed, he can sleep with you. He's got bad hips."

"How old is he?" Bailey asked.

"Just turned ten." Graham sounded like he'd gargled with sandpaper, his voice rough and low.

"I'll take her up, if you want," Annie said, a pure smile on her face. Laney couldn't help wondering if the woman had gotten some sort of weird idea about her and Graham.

Bailey got up and put her hand in Annie's, much to Laney's surprise.

Fighting exhaustion and thinking of those eighteen steps, Laney said, "Be sure to brush your teeth, Bay."

The little girl gave Laney a kiss and said, "Come on, dogs," before going with Annie. All three dogs jumped to their feet and followed, making Laney smile in appreciation for the canines.

"You love dogs," Graham said.

Laney let out the sigh she'd been holding in. "I do." She looked at Graham fully again, hoping they wouldn't get locked in that strange stare-fest again. "What about you? Have you had Bear for his whole life?"

"He was my father's dog." The lines around his eyes tightened for a breath, and then he relaxed. "We really can go down to the theater room. It's much more comfortable."

Laney had no doubt about that, and it was with more than a little bit of uncertainty that she said, "All right," and stood to follow him to a set of steps off the dining room that led into basement. Or would it be a dungeon?

The beast and his lair, she thought with an internal chuckle as she descended the steps behind his broad shoulders.

CHAPTER 6

Graham had no idea what he was doing. He only knew he couldn't stand to be confined to his bedroom or his office. And in a house as large as the lodge, he shouldn't have to. It was a rare bit of luck—or maybe God had truly answered his prayer—that he'd been able to get Laney alone without making a big deal of it or turning it into something awkward.

He hadn't exactly been on top of the dating game lately, and he wasn't even sure what movies he owned.

"What do you like?" he asked.

"I'm sorry?"

Just the sound of Laney's voice sent goose bumps across his skin. *Blast Bonnie*, he thought, not for the first time. But he couldn't really blame her, and he knew it. Maybe she'd just awakened the dormant feelings he had for Laney, made them come into the light, forced him to recognize them.

Problem was, he didn't know what to *do* about them. Dating in Seattle hadn't been this hard. He could meet someone for coffee or catch them on the coding floor. But here, going to town was a national event for him. He did it rarely except for church, and no one there had even remotely interested him.

Probably because someone has already caught your eye, he thought as he picked up the remote control and turned on the projector mounted in the ceiling. "Movies," he clarified. "What kind of movies do you like? What do you want to watch?"

"Oh, I don't care. You choose."

He faced her, the beauty in her face stunning him for a moment though he'd seen her hundreds of times. Had she always been this pretty?

"I'll probably just fall asleep," he said with a smile.

She laughed. "Me too."

"So maybe we don't want to watch a movie." The blue screen bloomed to life, casting eerie shadows on them in the dark theater room. He pressed another button on the remote and the lights brightened in slow degrees until the bulbs were at about half power.

Laney tucked her feet underneath her as she snuggled into one of the recliners. She looked up at him, an edge in her eye he could only classify as flirtatious. He frowned. That couldn't be it. maybe she didn't feel well after eating all that salad. Or something.

"You okay?" she asked.

"Yeah." He set the remote down and sat in the recliner next to hers. "Yeah." He ran both hands down his face.

"Just tired. It's been a busy day."

"Do you ever take time off?"

"Not usually," he said. "I try to work as little as possible on the Sabbath. Sometimes things come up."

"I always have ranch work on the Sabbath."

"But you go to church every week."

Her eyebrows flinched upward for only half a breath. "Yes. It's important to me that Bailey go. Plus, I like…I like going to church." She watched him, somehow taking more than he wanted to give her. "Do you like church?"

"Well enough. It makes my mother happy, and it forces me to slow down." Graham couldn't believe he'd revealed so much about himself. What he really wanted to tell her was that running this company was going to kill him.

He'd wanted to learn everything he could about Springside Energy, so he'd taken control of everything. The general manager, Dwight Rogers, pushed him on everything, and Graham was tired of fighting with the man.

Tired of looking at data. Tired of working in a stale office that smelled like last week's pizza. He missed the vibrancy of creating new programs, of experimenting with exciting technology, of the younger crowd who worked on his floor and brought in their strange clothing trends, their thick-framed glasses, and their innovative ideas.

His job in Seattle had kept him young, and here, he felt old. He felt like his father.

Laney's fingers landed on the back of his hand, branding him. A shock sparked between them and turned into slow heat the longer she kept her hand there.

Slowly, he lifted his eyes to hers. She had to feel the

same thing he did. Didn't she? No way this jolt, this fire between them, could be one-sided.

"I lost you," she said. "I asked you how your brothers were doing."

"Oh." He shook his head. "They're doing fine. Great. You'll get to see them all in a few days."

She looked at him with fondness in her gaze. "Remember when we all piled in that two-seater of your dad's? Six people for two seat belts." She chuckled, and Graham's memories streamed through his mind.

"I know I kept getting kneed in the back." He laughed too. "And that Sheriff Barnaby knew we were up to no good, even if he didn't pull us over."

"Great fishing that day, though." Laney smiled, and it held so much happiness. Happiness from easier times, lazier days, a more charmed life. "I remember you caught a rainbow trout and acted like it was the white whale."

Graham tipped his head back and laughed, a full belly laugh that sent endorphins and joy straight through his blood. "The white whale." He shook his head as he finished chuckling. "I don't remember you catching anything."

"That's because *someone* wouldn't help me bait the hook." She swatted at his hand, another touch that made him feel drunk with pleasure.

"And that's because someone who's seventeen years old should be able to bait their own hook." He grinned at her, relieved this flirty conversation was so easy.

Laney lifted her chin a fraction of an inch. "Fishing never was my thing."

"Obviously." He watched her for a moment, wondering if he could flip his hand over and hold hers. "But ranching is. You were born for that. Remember how you used to tell me that?"

Turn your hand over, he coached himself. She was obviously holding hers in place against the back of his. And yet, he couldn't make himself do it.

"I remember." Her eyes glittered like emerald stars, and Graham employed all his bravery and slowly turned his hand over, his knuckles bumping against her fingertips. Still, she didn't pull her hand away.

It seemed like ages had passed before he lined his fingers up with hers and laced their hands together. He met her eyes and found acceptance there, with an edge of heat that definitely testified that she wanted to hold his hand as much as he wanted to hold hers.

"All right, then," he murmured, and she ducked her head to hide a smile curving her lips. He caught it though, and a thrill shot all the way down to his toes.

"Tell me about what you have planned for Christmas," she said, and Graham groaned.

"Can't we just sit here and hold hands and take a nap?" he asked.

"It's almost nine o'clock." She giggled. "If you're tired, you should go to bed."

He leaned back in the recliner, closed his eyes, and squeezed her hand. "Too early. Just a little nap...." He opened one eye and gave her a wicked grin. "You can tell me more memories from our teen years."

"Oh, I can't do that."

He looked at her fully now. "Why not?"

She looked uncomfortable and lifted her shoulders in a shrug. "I don't know. I just can't."

"Tell me about your ex, then."

"Hard pass."

So there was a history there. Of course there was. She'd married someone and had a kid with them.

"Why did you come to Coral Canyon?" she asked.

"My father died," he said.

"Yeah, but he had a general manager. You didn't have to stay."

No, he didn't. "I felt a sense of obligation," he said, saying something he hadn't told anyone before. "And I needed a change of scenery."

"Oh? You didn't like living in Seattle?"

"You knew I lived in Seattle?" He stayed reclined, but he turned his head toward her.

"It's a small town," she said. "When someone from one of the wealthiest families leaves, everyone knows where they are."

Graham detected a small untruth in the statement, but he accepted it anyway. "Fair enough."

"What did you do there, anyway?"

"Computer science," he said. "I was the developmental team leader for new production."

"Wow, sounds fancy. And made up." She gave him a coy smile, and he shook his head as if in disbelief.

"That was the official title. We made productivity apps for robots. Lettucebot came out of my department."

"I have no idea what you're talking about."

"I worked to make everyday tasks easier for people in a wide variety of professions. Everything from fashion, to energy, to farming. Lettucebot can analyze hundreds of thousands of lettuce plants and inform farmers how to improve their productivity and crops while spending less money." He tried to keep the pride from his voice, but he'd loved his job in Seattle.

"You sound like you enjoyed it." Laney was nothing if not perceptive, and Graham should've known better. She'd always been able to pin down exactly what he thought and felt even when he hadn't said things very explicitly.

"I did."

"But you still needed a change?"

He didn't know how much to say about his departure from Seattle—and why he'd done it—and how much to keep to himself. "My dad died just after Christmas." He shrugged. "It was a good time to leave. Start fresh."

She reached over with her free hand and brushed his hair off his forehead. The gesture felt wildly intimate and he stared at her, sure all of his feelings were plain to see on his face.

"You don't look that fresh," she said. "Do you even like running Springside Energy?"

His first inclination was to say that of course he liked running the family company. But the truth was, he'd found the whole thing tedious and overwhelming. "It's not bad," he hedged. "Just busier than I thought."

She studied him and finally said, "I think you might be choosing that."

He closed his eyes again. "I probably am." But there

was no probably about it. In fact, Graham had the distinct thought that he made everything harder than it had to be, including starting something with Laney.

Why couldn't they hold hands and help each other on their farms and ranches? Why couldn't he kiss her and still be her best friend?

"Hey, Laney?" he asked, deciding to do something instead of just think about it until his thoughts drove him mad.

"Yeah?"

"When the roads are clear, would you like to go to dinner with me?" He didn't dare open his eyes to see her reaction.

Several long seconds passed before she said, "Yeah, I think that would be nice."

Graham's smile felt like the first genuine thing he'd done in a while, and he squeezed her hand, glad when she squeezed back.

CHAPTER 7

Laney slept later than she had in years. When she woke, the bed beneath her felt foreign, and she sat straight up, wondering why her alarm hadn't gone off or why Bailey hadn't gotten her up to go feed the horses.

The glass to her left rattled, and she glanced in that direction. The storm beyond it still howled, and everything rushed back at her. The blizzard. The power going out. The dinner, the hand-holding, the conversation at the lodge.

She lay back against the pillows again, a slow smile touching her lips. Could it be that Graham truly liked her?

"He asked you to dinner," Laney reminded herself, as if she hadn't repeated the question to herself a dozen times last night as she tried to fall asleep. And then her dreams had featured the two of them as they danced and dined, laughed and lunched. Heck, she'd even imagined a coffee date with him in the morning, which was absolutely ridiculous as she never had time in the morning to simply sit around and sip coffee.

Except for today, as apparently she wasn't going to be doing any chores. She felt the weight she normally carried drift off her shoulders, and it was warm and wonderful to just have nothing to do, nothing to stress about, nothing to divide her attention.

She grabbed her phone from the nightstand and checked the clock. Almost eight-thirty. She flung the blankets off though she wanted to stay in bed for a while longer, and pulled her hoodie over her pajamas.

"Bailey?" She opened her door and found the one across from her ajar as well. Great, her daughter was up and who-knows-where. Trepidation tugged through her and she moved down the hall to the banister so she could see into the foyer. The scent of cinnamon and yeast met her nose and made her stomach growl. But she couldn't hear anything.

"The dogs," she muttered, wondering where they'd gotten to. Hopefully Bailey had fed them, and hopefully Graham didn't mind that Laney had taken the liberty to shirk pretty much all of her duties. She hoped he didn't think this was how she always acted.

She hustled down the steps, around the massive Christmas tree that seemed a bit ominous without any lights or ornaments or decoration of any kind, and through the archway that led into the kitchen and dining room.

There, she found Annie showing Bailey how to cut cinnamon rolls with a piece of dental floss that Laney hoped was unwaxed and unscented. They both wore aprons, and Bailey's hair had been plaited into two braids that ran down the sides of her head.

Laney stared, wondering how on earth Annie had done the braids. Laney was hopeless with things like that, and Bailey wore her hair in a ponytail most days.

Bailey caught sight of her and said, "Mom." She danced over to her and took her hand. "Come see what we're making."

Laney's feet felt like someone had filled them with lead, but she managed to move over to the stretch of counter where Annie worked. "I'm so sorry," she said. "I overslept."

"It's no problem." Annie flashed her a smile. "We've been up for what?" She grinned at Bailey. "Maybe forty-five minutes."

"Look at my hair, Mom." Bailey's whole face had come alive, and Laney couldn't remember the last time she'd seen her daughter so flushed, so happy, so engaged. She usually watched TV or played on her tablet so Laney could cook dinner, or work on the ranch. Sometimes when she played with the barn dogs in the summer, she looked like she was enjoying herself.

It had never occurred to Laney to involve Bailey in the cooking, but the girl watched with rapt attention as Annie drew the floss through the dough. Bailey picked up the slice and put it on the sheet tray with the others.

"And we're making cinnamon rolls. Annie says it's her mother's recipe."

Then it would be good. Susannah Pruitt had won the town picnic baking contest several times. Maybe not with cinnamon rolls, but with honey wheat bread, lemon zucchini bread, and Laney's personal favorite—oatmeal raisin cookies.

"Your hair is beautiful." Laney touched one loop of the braid, still not sure how Annie had done it. "And I love cinnamon rolls."

"I fed the dogs," Bailey said, picking up another slice after Annie cut it. "And Graham said to let you sleep as long as you want."

A dose of heat filled her, and she hoped she didn't blush too furiously. "Where is he?" she asked, knowing Bailey wouldn't hear anything in her voice but suspecting that Annie would.

"Probably the office," Annie said. "That's where he always is when I come."

"How often do you clean?" Laney asked.

"Twice a week," she said. "Sometimes three times if Graham's having a...messy week." She paused in the cutting of the dough and glanced over Bailey's head to Laney. "He's not the neatest person on the planet. So if it's rainy weather or something like that, I come more often."

Laney gave her a smile and she went back to pulling the floss. So Graham wasn't very clean. Neither was Laney, if the piles of paper around her house were any indication.

"Do you think he would mind if I went to say good morning?"

That got Annie to come to a full stop, mid-slice even. "At your peril," she said, her eyes wide. "He doesn't allow anyone in the office."

"I'll just lean in the doorway." Laney put her arm around Bailey and gave her a side hug. "Love you, bug."

"Love you too, Momma."

With that, Laney left the two of them in the kitchen and went through the length of the kitchen to find a mudroom on her right, where the dog food bowls waited and at least a dozen jackets, sweatshirts, and coats hung on pegs. Three pairs of work boots sat on the floor, none of them clean, along with an assortment of sneakers and hiking shoes.

To her left, and through another arch, she went down a hall with several doors leading from it. She assumed a couple to be closets, but she saw a bathroom before she came to a door almost all the way closed.

The scent of something sweet met her nose, but she wasn't sure if she wanted to know the source of it. "Knock, knock," she said at the same time she rapped on the wood. Everything in the lodge had been done with the finest materials, and though she'd barely touched it, the door swung in a little.

Laney stepped to the other side of the doorway and looked inside. "Graham?"

Music filled the air now and she found his silhouette way across the office, standing with his back to her as he gazed out the window. She didn't recognize the song playing, but that wasn't unusual. She had little time for pop culture and rarely listened to music.

Graham knew it though, and well enough to sing along with the lyrics. His voice, a beautiful rich tenor, lifted into the air and sent chills down her spine and across her shoulders. She wasn't even sure what he said, because the richness of his singing was so stunning.

The song ended, and Laney couldn't help clapping her hands. When someone sang like that, they deserved a standing ovation.

Graham spun from the window, his face a mask of anger. "What are you doing?" He took long strides across the office, his frown so deep Laney thought she'd fall into it and never get out.

"I just came to say good morning." Laney fell back a step, sure Graham would plow right into her, bodily removing her from his office though she hadn't stepped a single toe inside yet.

He froze as if someone had encased his feet in liquid nitrogen. His fury smoothed away, and he glanced around the office and back to her, his face holding a bit of a flush it hadn't a few moments ago.

"Laney," he said as if he'd just remembered her name.

"Graham." She smiled and stepped forward again— still not entering the office. "I didn't mean to surprise you. I heard you singing. It was beautiful."

He ducked his head though he wore no cowboy hat on that morning. She liked him with it and without it, his dark hair falling across his forehead. She had the strongest urge to reach up and brush it back, but she kept her hands resolutely at her sides.

She glanced around the office, and it indeed could use a housekeeper. "You're a stacker."

"Hmm?" He lifted his eyes to hers, and she indicated the office.

"A stacker. A piler. I make all sorts of piles. My ex—" Her voice cut off for a moment, but she forced herself to go on. "Mike used to poke fun at me about it all the time." She lifted her chin. "But I knew where everything was. And if I didn't, I knew it was in one of my piles."

"Is that right?" Graham softened when he smiled, and Laney's heart melted.

"I didn't mean to oversleep today," she said.

"And I didn't mean to come stomping across the office."

"I could help you tidy it up."

He frowned again. "It's fine. I'm wondering, though, if you'd help me assign rooms to all the guests."

Laney's eyebrows went up. "Isn't it just your brothers coming in?"

"I wish." Graham ran his hand through his hair. "My mother is coming to stay for a few days, even though she lives in town. Same with Beau. And yes, Andrew and Eli are coming. But Andrew's bringing his assistant —a woman—and she needs her own room. Or somewhere to share with someone. And Eli's bringing a couple of friends who didn't have anywhere else to go for the holidays, along with his nanny and his five-year-old son."

"I didn't know Eli had a son."

"Yeah." Graham exhaled and ran his hands through his hair. "His wife died a couple of years ago in an accident. Eli does...well, Eli's doing the best he can, just like all of us."

"Where is he living?"

"He's in Bora Bora right now. Runs a big resort and spa down there."

"Oh, he's going to love the snow, then." Laney laughed, glad when Graham softened enough to chuckle too.

"All right. So the guests." Laney mentally counted. Four brothers. A mother. Five others. "That's only ten people," she said. "You've got what? At least that many bedrooms here?" She'd been downstairs last night, but she hadn't gotten a grand tour or anything.

"Twelve," he said, waving his hand toward the far wall. "Plus mine."

"So plenty of room."

"Celia's coming tonight to cook for the rest of the holidays," he said.

"Really?" Laney took a chance and stepped into the office. "Can she get through the storm?"

"It's supposed to let up for a few hours this afternoon." Graham turned away from her and drifted further into the office, leaving Laney to follow him if she so chose.

She did, and she wanted to hold his hand again, so she took slow, careful steps after him and slipped her hand into his, hoping whatever was troubling him would ease with the human contact.

He dipped his chin and looked at their joined hands, then looked at her. She gazed back, not afraid to let him know she was interested.

"Take me on a tour," she said. "I'll help you make room assignments. Bailey will probably make nameplates if you want her to." She smiled, glad when some of his melancholy evaporated right then and there.

"Yeah?"

"Oh, yeah. She loves to color. Of course, you're going to have to tear her from the cinnamon rolls they're baking, but I bet she has time." She giggled, and when he added his chuckle to the sound, it made the most beautiful harmony.

"All right." He swept his lips along her temple, leaving behind a trail of fire, and added, "Let's go take a tour."

CHAPTER 8

G raham held Laney's hand in the doorway of the office and checked both directions like he'd snuck a girl into his bedroom and wanted to get her out of the house before his parents found out.

"My room's down there," he said, indicating the door at the end of the hall. "Around the corner, there are two more bedrooms. I was thinking my mother should stay in one of them."

"Do I get to see them?"

He didn't want to show her his mess, but the other bedrooms held clean linens and scented candles, so he figured they were safe. He led her that way, bypassing his room and entering the one kitty-corner across the hall from his.

"This room is somewhat small. Maybe no one will stay here if we can help it." The door settled open to reveal more of the cream-colored walls the rest of the main floor boasted, with white wainscoting along the lower third. His interior designer had done this room in cool colors, with peach and robin egg blue as the dominant palette.

The queen bed took most of the room, but a small dresser held a TV. Graham stared at it in distaste. Why was there a TV in this room, where not a single person had ever stayed?

"This is nice." Laney beamed up at him, but Graham kept his attention on the bedroom.

"The other one is bigger." He led her to it and stepped all the way inside. This one held a queen bed too, with two recliners flanking the window. "There's a bathroom between them," he said. "I guess sort of a family suite type of setup."

"Your mother would like this one." Laney ran her free fingertips along the surface of the bedside table and added, "I like the seashells. Did you pick those out?"

"Heavens, no." He snorted and laughed. "Surely you know by now that I pay for things I don't want to deal with or don't know how to do."

"So which is this one?" She gestured to the room. "Don't want to deal with, or don't know how to do?"

He surveyed the room, with the lighthouse artwork, the seaman's rope on the wall beside it, and all the other nautical trimmings. "Both."

Laney laughed, the sound delicious to his ears, and he smiled down at her. Their eyes locked, and the moment between them lengthened and lengthened. Graham's thoughts turned to kissing, and his gaze dropped to her mouth.

Those full lips taunted him, especially when she licked them and swallowed as if nervous. He was just about to lean down and see how far she'd let him go when she said, "Should we go downstairs?"

He jerked back, her message loud and clear in his ears. "Yeah." His voice sounded like it belonged to a grumpy bear, and he dropped her hand as he stepped out of the bedroom. He would've anyway, as soon as they'd approached the kitchen. This was just a couple of hallways and a turn earlier than he'd anticipated doing it.

The basement felt cold and lonely, though he'd been down here just last night. The four bedrooms down here should probably be the bachelor pad for Andrew, Eli, and his friends, and Laney agreed.

"The nanny can stay upstairs with the assistant," Laney said.

"And we'll give Eli and his son a room to themselves. The others can share."

In addition to the four bedrooms and two bathrooms, the basement was home to a theater room, a second, much smaller kitchen, and a game room with a pool table, air hockey, and vintage video game console.

Graham had no use for any of it. The double-wide doors led out of the game room and into the backyard, but a mountain of snow pressed against the glass, and no one would be exiting that way during this holiday season.

"So that just leaves your brother's assistant," Laney said as they climbed the steps to the main floor. "What's down there?" She pointed to the couple of doors past the kitchen.

"That one goes into the garage," he said. "The other one is a utility room. Washer, dryer, that sort of thing."

"How functional," she said, and Graham wasn't sure if she really didn't want the lodge tour or not.

"And you've seen upstairs," he said, deciding to end it here. "I'm sure we'll be fine."

"We?" Laney faced him, a definite challenge in her eyes now. "You mean you'll be fine."

"You're coming, aren't you?"

"Coming for dinner isn't the same as staying over."

"It's more than dinner," he said. "I've already told Bailey about the tree lighting ceremony, and she seemed excited." His heart shriveled with every second where she didn't confirm she would bring Bailey to every event he'd planned for the holidays.

"We'll have to see," Laney said, as he'd suspected she would. "I have a ranch to run, and with the snow, it'll be ten times as much work as it normally is." A measure of exhaustion passed through her eyes, and Graham wanted to erase it for her.

"I'll come help," he said.

She laughed, this sound only half as cheery as previously. "I've seen you do farm work," she said. "I'm probably better off without you."

"Ouch." He grinned at her and tucked a piece of hair behind her ear. "What just happened there?"

"Where?"

"In the basement. Between the basement and here."

Her eyes darted away, toward the garage, and then

came back to his. "It's just...I mean, I knew you had a lot of money."

"Mm hm." Graham didn't want to talk about money, especially his.

"How much do you have, exactly?"

"Why does it matter?"

Laney's features hardened, and she said, "It doesn't. I'm sorry. I shouldn't have asked."

And suddenly Graham wanted to tell her. He checked the kitchen but couldn't see or hear Bailey or Annie. "When my father died, his fortune largely went to my mother. Us boys each got a piece, and...."

Laney slipped her hand into Graham's again and strolled toward the foyer. He waited until they were steadily climbing the steps before he said, "I run the company, so I got a bigger share. It's...big." Why couldn't he say it out loud?

Laney didn't ask, and he told himself that if she did, he'd tell her.

"Would you say we're friends?" she asked.

He lifted their joined hands. "I'd say so."

She gave a tight smile. "I'd say you're my best friend." Her voice could barely be heard, though the rest of the house sat in silence. "Just like in high school and all growing up."

"Those were good times."

"The best."

Graham took a deep breath. "Laney, you're my best friend too." He tightened his grip on her fingers. "Which is why I wasn't sure I should do this."

"Have you thought about it long?"

"Long enough." He'd gotten good at saying nothing over the course of the last year. Most people didn't demand a straight answer, and Laney was one of them.

"So my ranch is barely staying afloat," she said. "I'm doing the best I can, but sometimes it's lean."

Graham immediately wanted to help her, but he knew Laney would refuse. And probably stop holding his hand. And talking to him. She was beautiful and kind, but stubborn and hard-working too. She would not take his charity, even if he tried to give it to her anonymously.

"I have nine zeroes in my bank account," he said as they reached the first door at the top of the steps, the room where Annie had been staying.

Laney chuckled. "Ah, so I have a cowboy billionaire best friend. Good to know."

"Well, I wouldn't really call myself a cowboy."

"You have the hat."

"Is that all it takes?"

"Around these parts?" Laney glanced at him, a playful expression on her face. "I'd say so."

He gave a light laugh and tucked her into his side, realizing that was right where he wanted her to be.

———

WORKING TOGETHER, HE AND LANEY GOT HIS HORSES TAKEN care of and went down to her ranch too. She had a lot more animals than he did, but they all seemed to have come through the worst of the storm all right.

They checked blankets and filled troughs. The barn dogs had a cozy room where they holed up, and she put three times as much food as they needed. Without the heaters, the chickens hadn't fared so well.

"Oh, no." Laney picked up one frozen bird. "Bailey will be so upset. She's named them all. It's her job to feed the chickens."

"Let's move the rest of them into the barn." They did, the work hard through the snow and the gray sky and the cold. With everything taken care of, she checked the house and came out only a few minutes later.

"Still no power," she called to him, a worried look on her face. "I'm going to pack another bag. Can we stay with you?"

"Of course." He kept the broad smile off his face but felt the warmth spreading through his whole body.

"I'll make Bailey come sleep with me," she said. "We won't take up two of your bedrooms."

"It's fine," he said. "By my count, we only need one more room upstairs, and we have three." He gazed at her, wondering how to help her. "Besides, they're not coming in for another day anyway."

"I'll call about the power tomorrow," she said, glancing back toward her house. "I don't know why I didn't call today." She faced him again. "My pipes are all going to be frozen."

"The power company wouldn't have been able to come anyway." Graham hadn't thought of it either, and the fact was, he liked having Laney and Bailey upstairs, and he hoped they might be able to stay for several more days. He looked up into the sky. "It's just starting to clear up."

"And the forecast says it's supposed to snow overnight." Laney heaved a big sigh and spread her arms wide to the sky. She turned in a circle and said, "Remember when we used to shout what we wanted into the sky?"

Graham remembered, but he didn't want to play that game right now. Because he was looking at what he wanted, and he wasn't sure he could censor himself if she insisted he bellow to the clouds the way they had as eighth graders.

"What are you gonna yell?" He watched her, her presence so strong as she twirled in the snow, her boots crunching it down.

She came to a stop and faced him, a giant grin on her face. He returned the smile, her happiness almost infectious, and the electric charges in his pulse testified that his feelings for her weren't because Bonnie had put the idea in his head to ask her out.

"Why did we never go out before?" he asked, cocking his head.

Her smile slipped, and Graham did some major backpedaling. "I mean, I was dating...someone. What was her name?" And why couldn't he remember it?

"Emma Darrow," Laney said immediately. "She married Flynn Mason, you know."

"I think I heard that." A long, long time ago. She probably had children the same age he was last time he'd thought about Emma.

"And we never dated because we weren't that kind of friends." Laney folded her arms as if hugging herself to keep warm.

Graham took a step toward her and then another one. "Are we that kind of friends now?" He ran his gloved hands from her elbows to her shoulders and back down, really hoping she'd say yes.

"I think we should probably define what kind of friends we are," she said, a shaky note in her voice on the last few words. "What with your family coming into town and all."

Graham nodded, but he didn't open his mouth to make any such definitions.

"Oh, you want me to start?" Her eyes crinkled as she smiled and shook her head. "Always making me do the heavy lifting."

"Hey, I got down all the hay to feed the horses over here." He grinned at her.

"Yes, well." She put her hands on his biceps and squeezed, though she surely couldn't feel anything through his thick, winter coat. "These muscles should be good for so much more than that."

"Different kind of lifting," he said, still wanting her to begin. She seemed interested in him, and he wondered how long she'd thought of him as a man she'd like to go to dinner with. Hold hands with. Maybe even kiss….

"I had a crush on you in high school," she said with a swallow. "Did you know?"

Graham blinked, sure he'd heard her wrong. "I had no

idea." Foolishness raced through him at the speed of light. "You never acted like it."

She lifted one shoulder in a shrug and Graham dropped his hands to her waist. The desire to kiss her soared toward the heavens as she laid her cheek against his chest and exhaled. "You always had Emma, and I always knew you'd leave Coral Canyon. I'm actually surprised you're back." She leaned away from him and searched his face. "You're planning to stay, right?"

If he wanted to keep those nine zeroes. "Yes," he said. "I'm planning to stay."

Laney looked like she didn't quite believe him, but she nodded.

"So," he said.

A flirtatious twinkle entered her light eyes, making them sparkle like gems. "So what?"

"So you tell me what kind of friends we are so I can decide what to do next."

"What do you want to do next?"

He swallowed, finding his throat very, very dry. "Do I have to yell it into the sky?"

She shook her head slowly as if she knew exactly what he wanted, the ends of her hair brushing the backs of his gloves.

"No," she said slowly. "You can whisper it to me if you want."

He bent down, taking a careful breath of the scent of her hair, her skin. He got something soft mixed with something fruity, and the combination of smells nearly drove him to madness.

"I want to kiss you," he whispered, his lips danger-ously close to her earlobe.

She shivered in his arms, and he hoped it wasn't all because of the cold temperatures. "All right."

He pulled back slightly so he could see her face. "All right?"

She nodded, and Graham switched his gaze to those lips that had tormented him for a full twenty-four hours. He lowered his head toward her, thrilled when she stretched up on her toes. Inch by inch, he closed the distance between them, sure he was about to kiss her.

"Wait," she said, planting one hand on his chest.

He froze, waiting, but she said nothing.

CHAPTER 9

Laney's heart thundered against her ribs like she was about to go over a steep set of falls in a boat with no lifejacket.

"I—" she started, only to have her voice fail her.

"It's okay." Graham started to retreat from her, physically and emotionally, and she hated that. Wanted him right beside her, confiding in her, helping her on this ranch.

"No," she said quickly, her grip tightening on his one shoulder and moving her hand from his chest to behind his neck. "Don't go."

"What is it?"

She liked that he wasn't demanding but still wanted to know. Those dark eyes searched hers, full of compassion and hunger and a pinch of frustration.

"I haven't kissed a man in a long time," she blurted out. "I've been divorced for three years, and it was over long before that." She licked her lips, wishing her salivary glands hadn't gone on vacation during this conversation.

Graham's expression filled with kindness. "And you think you've forgotten how?"

She lifted that one shoulder again. "Maybe."

"How about we try it and I'll let you know?" His eyes glinted with danger now, with need.

She giggled. "I sort of feel like I've ruined the moment."

"Not at all." He dipped his head and ran the tip of his nose along her cheek, his lips touching the soft skin just behind her jawbone. She sucked in a breath and gripped his shoulders tighter.

If he kissed her, she felt sure she wouldn't even be able to stay standing. Heat filled her body, making her feel like she was steaming in the sub-zero temperatures.

Graham kneaded her closer, and she'd spent a lot of time thinking about what kissing him would be like, so when he finally touched his lips to hers, she knew exactly what to expect.

At least she thought she did.

An explosion of fire burst through her, and she lifted onto her toes to make his feather light touch stronger. She matched him stroke for stroke, and she knew that all of her fantasies as a teenager were way off the mark.

So were the dreams she'd had this past year.

Because kissing Graham was so much better than anything she could've imagined.

Several seconds passed before he broke the connection

just long enough to murmur, "You still know how to do it, Laney," before kissing her again.

————

LANEY SORT OF FLOATED BACK TO THE LODGE, NOT FEELING the bite of the winter air until she was back inside where it was warm and she could appreciate how cold it had been outside.

"Mom, I helped Annie make lunch."

"Hmm?" Laney looked down at the blonde angel before her, taking an extra moment to recognize the girl as her daughter. "Is it lunchtime already?"

"It was an hour ago," Annie said, still wearing the apron from that morning. She put both hands on her hips and also wore a knowing expression.

Laney's stomach grumbled. "I am hungry."

"Me too." Graham arranged his boots on the drying mat in the mudroom where he'd hung his coat too. "You didn't have to make anything, Annie. There're leftovers in the fridge."

"Miss Bailey wanted grilled cheese sandwiches." The redhead gazed fondly at Bailey and tousled her hair. "She did a great job with buttering the bread."

Once again, guilt flowed through Laney with the force of river rapids. If they were still in their home, Bailey probably would've eaten cold cereal or a PB&J for lunch. Laney would've talked to her about it before she went out to do the chores, and she wouldn't feel this pinch of guilt behind her heart that someone else had been taking care of her child while she kissed a handsome man by the barn.

The ghost of that kiss still lingered on her lips, but she refused to let her hands drift up to touch them.

"I'll heat something up," Graham said, completely oblivious to Laney's inner turmoil. Of course he was. Bailey wasn't his daughter, and even if she was, he wouldn't feel the same. She knew from personal experience.

Mike had often told her she had too soft of a heart, that Bailey needed to be raised with love but that disappointment, chores, and hard times were okay too.

Well, she'd had plenty of experience with all of the above since he'd walked out on them.

"Roast beef from last night?" Graham held up a plastic container. "Or orange chicken with brown rice?"

"Orange chicken," Laney said, pushing the guilt back and letting her interest in the food take over. "Who makes their own orange chicken? I thought you could only get that from The Magic Noodle."

Graham made a face. "The Magic Noodle isn't even good." He cracked the lid on the container and stuck it in the microwave.

"Mom likes the teriyaki noodles."

"I love noodles," Laney admitted with a shrug and a smile. "And I'm not driving sixty minutes round-trip to Jackson for Chu's, though it is better." But if she had that kind of time and money, she wouldn't have been praying all these weeks for God to send her a miracle.

As she watched Graham bustle around his kitchen,

pulling out plates and silverware so they could eat, she wondered if the Lord had answered her prayers—just not in the way she'd thought they should be answered.

The rest of the day passed, with Bailey making name-plates for everyone coming into town while Laney super-vised. Annie left sometime in the early evening, and Celia arrived with bags and bags of groceries.

Laney made herself useful, not quite sure what to do with empty hours. She was so used to having dozens of items on her to-do list and never quite crossing them all off. Sitting at the kitchen table while her daughter colored and she did nothing...well, Laney thought she might go mad if she had to do it for much longer.

Celia was her mother's age, and a lifelong resident of Coral Canyon herself, so Laney donned the apron Annie had been wearing earlier that day, washed her hands, and said, "Put me to work, Celia," with a smile that was prob-ably one part friendliness and two parts overeager.

"Can you peel carrots and potatoes?" Celia kept unpacking the groceries.

"Yes, ma'am."

She pointed to a ten-pound bag of russets. "All of those." She slapped a bag of carrots about half as big. "And these."

While peeling potatoes wasn't high on Laney's list of fun things to spend her time doing, she picked up the peeler and got to work. "What are you making?"

"Beef stew," she said. "Chicken pot pie. French toast breakfast casserole. Lasagna. Stuff Graham can put in the oven and serve with rolls or bagged salad or fruit."

"I don't think he eats fruit." Laney sent long strips of brown skins into the sink.

Celia laughed, the sound filling the kitchen with more life than Laney had felt in years. She smiled at the older woman.

"You're probably right about that." She finished chuckling and folded the reusable grocery bags. "But I heard there will be women and children here, and they should probably have access to something that isn't brown."

"Agreed." She set the peeled potatoes in a pot of water so they wouldn't discolor until Celia needed them.

She banged around the kitchen with ease, and Laney asked, "How long have you been cooking for Graham?"

"About seven months now," she said. "You should've seen him when I first showed up." She shook her head and clucked her tongue. "I thought he was going to waste away."

Laney laughed, realizing too late that the other woman wasn't kidding. "I saw him when he first moved here. He seemed fine." Fine enough to call her every other day about a problem for those first couple of months.

"If you think he doesn't eat vegetables now, you should've seen him when he hired me." Celia pointed the tip of her knife in Laney's direction though they stood yards apart. "I got him on vitamins and he's perked right up."

Yeah, perky was how Laney would describe him too. She shook her head at the assessment, a wry smile curving her lips. "How's your daughter?" she asked, deciding Graham was dangerous territory for a conversation with someone as keen as Celia Armstrong. She practically ran the gossip mill in town, and Laney didn't need her name circulating through the salons and church functions.

"Oh, Diana's fine," she said. "She's got her hands full with the twins. They've been acting up since their dad was diagnosed."

"And how is Devon?" Laney felt a tug of sorrow pull through her. Diana and Devon had been through so much together already. It didn't seem fair that he had to deal with cancer now, too, after all they'd gone through to get their babies.

"About as expected." The swish of the knife went through onions and celery, and Celia came over to get the peeled carrots. "The cancer hasn't spread, but it's not shrinking either." She gave Laney a sad smile. "At least the twins can drive now, so Diana doesn't have to do so much arranging when they have to go to the hospital for treatments."

Laney remembered the sign-up sheet that had gone around at church for months to help get the twins to school or from their activities on days Diana had to drive Devon to his treatment sessions, an hour and a half away.

She never had been able to sign up and help, because it was twenty minutes just to get from the ranch to town, and she had her own daughter to take care of. At least that was how she'd justified not signing up.

"So," Celia said, and Laney's defenses went right up at the tone. There was just something about it. Something that said she was about to pry.

"Will you be staying at Whiskey Mountain for the holidays?"

"Oh, no." Laney laughed, again the only one to do so, which made it awkward. "No. I'm just here until the power comes back on at my place."

"Your power is off?"

Laney glanced up. "Yes."

Celia frowned and went back to cubing meat. "I haven't heard of any power outages."

"I have private lines that hook to the county," Laney said. "I'm sure I just need someone to come look at them." At least she hoped so. She didn't need another bill, or another worry to add to the ones she already had about the animals freezing, or the pipes bursting, or how she'd explain to Bailey that Santa would find them here at the lodge if they couldn't get home in time for Christmas.

"How are you and Graham getting along?" Celia asked next, and Laney froze. The vegetables sizzled on the stove several paces away, where Celia worked, the scent of onions and butter so homey to Laney's nose.

"Fine," she took too long to say.

"Mm hm."

Laney glanced up in time to see the knowing look on Celia's face, almost like she could tell that Laney had experienced the best kiss of her life only hours ago.

"He's a bit of a beast, to be honest," Laney said, hoping to deflect some of the tension. "Don't you think?"

Celia laughed and dropped the meat in the pot, where it hissed when it hit the hot surface. She added a liberal amount of salt and pepper as she said, "He's tame-able, though. Has a good heart. You stick around long enough, and you'll see."

Laney had already seen that, but she did wonder if he knew how demanding he was, or how some of his "requests" came off.

Thankfully, Celia moved on to something else, some rumor that had been going around since Halloween, and Laney was able to barely listen as she relived the kiss over and over again.

CHAPTER 10

G raham pressed his back into the wall, the women's voices on the other side reaching his ears but the words like ribbons without sound.

He's a bit of a beast, to be honest.

Laney thought he was a beast?

His fingers curled into fists, clenching tight before releasing. So maybe he'd been a bit short with her in the past. Maybe. He couldn't actually remember being anything but himself, but that didn't really mean he hadn't come off as a beast.

A beast.

He couldn't believe she'd said that about him to his personal chef. But of course she knew Celia Armstrong, the original short-order cook at the diner in town for thirty-five years before retiring a few years ago.

What was he going to do now? He'd stepped down the hall to his office for a little bit, mostly to get re-centered after the bone-melting kiss he'd shared with Laney near her barn. Now he'd been hoping to get a few more private moments with her somehow.

He couldn't suggest a walk because of the weather, but he'd been planning to ask her to go around with him and hang the nameplates her daughter had made. So maybe he'd envisioned himself kissing her in the dim theater room, or around the corner in the hallway upstairs.

The beast got his kiss with Beauty, didn't he?

Maybe you've already gotten yours, he thought, his heart sinking all the way to the soles of his feet. And maybe he needed to be the forty-year-old he was and talk to her about everything from the kiss to why she thought he was a beast.

So he stepped around the wall to the delicious smell of Celia's beef stew and Laney washing her hands and saying, "What do you need next?"

"I was wondering if I could steal Laney for a few minutes." He flashed a smile that was certainly un-beastly at Celia. "She's helping me get the rooms ready for the guests."

Both women raised their eyebrows. Laney recovered first, taking a few extra seconds to wipe her hands on a towel and say, "Let me find Bailey."

"She gave me the nameplates," Graham said. "They're in the office. And I was hoping we could work on decorating the tree tonight and tomorrow too. I want to have the big lighting ceremony in the evening after everyone arrives."

"I thought you were going to have Bree do the decorating."

"She ran out of time," Graham said simply, hoping Celia wouldn't spill all the secrets he'd kept behind the closed doors of Whiskey Mountain Lodge. Laney didn't need to know that Bree had run out of time to decorate the twenty-foot Christmas tree in the foyer because Graham had given her the task of finding enough stockings for all the guests coming in and doing all of his gift shopping.

Bree had become somewhat of his personal assistant this winter, and he suddenly felt like a *beast* for not going down to town and buying his own brothers their gifts.

"I'm sure Bailey would love to do that," she said. "We don't even have a tree at home." She held his gaze for only a moment and then tucked her hands into her pockets.

The second stretched, with the three of them standing there in an awkward triangle. Finally, Celia said, "Well, go on then. I can manage just fine in here alone." She ping-ponged her gaze back and forth between Graham and Laney. "Probably better if no one's in my hair." She turned back to the large pot on the stove, leaving Graham nowhere to look but at Laney.

"Shall we?" He wanted to recall the words as soon as they left his mouth. This wasn't a date, and he didn't need to act like it was. Unsure of what else to say, he stepped out of the kitchen and started down the hall toward his office.

Celia caught him at the second arch—which also led into the kitchen, just on the other side where the mudroom was—a roll of clear tape in her hand. She didn't say anything but cocked one eyebrow at him and ducked back into the kitchen.

He collected the nameplates from his desk and rounded the corner to put up his mother's. The words he wanted to say, the questions he had to ask, seemed to pile on top of each other, unable to come out one at a time.

So he taped the rainbow-colored paper that said *Amanda* on it in all capital letters. "Bailey is really creative," he said.

"She is." Laney edged in a little closer, and he caught a whiff of her perfume.

He stepped back and over to the next door.

"I didn't think anyone was going to stay here," she said.

"Andrew requested a quiet wing for his assistant." He rolled his eyes as he tore off another piece of tape. "Apparently public relations personnel are always working, even at Christmastime."

"You don't sound happy about it."

He smoothed the tape so it would hold the sign with *Tilly* on it, little sea creatures floating in the ocean scene surrounding the letters.

"Oh, am I being a little bit like a beast?" He cast her a glare, lifted his eyebrows, and rounded the corner before she could respond. He'd taken three steps before he spun back, his pulse ricocheting around inside his chest. But he wasn't going to walk away.

Graham pulled up short when he found Laney only a pace behind him. "You know what?" he asked. "This year hasn't been easy for me. So maybe I've come off a little rough around the edges. Doesn't mean I'm a beast."

Her eyes blazed with something like lightning. "You were eavesdropping?"

"There are half a dozen entrances into that kitchen. I was walking by."

Her countenance fell. "I didn't mean anything by it." She put her palm flat against his breastbone, and dang if his heart didn't hammer faster. And she'd probably be able to feel it. "I just didn't want Celia to know about...you know."

"That we kissed," he said, not ashamed of it. Was she?

She grabbed onto his elbow and pulled him back around the corner, her eyes anxious and her grip firm. Somehow, it made his blood run hotter.

"Laney, did you not want me to kiss you?"

"No," she said. "I mean, yes." She exhaled and ran her palm over her hair, smoothing back the errant pieces.

"You just don't want anyone to know about it."

She looked up at him, the fire and strength he'd seen in her as a ten-year-old when she punched the bullies on the school bus who kept stealing her bubble gum blazing in those light green eyes.

He'd seen this determination when she entered the FFA competitions. And as she'd reprimanded him for trespassing on her property.

"Graham," she said in a freaky calm voice. "I have a six-year-old daughter. I've been married before. You'll forgive me if this needs to go...slow."

Graham wasn't sure how to answer. He also wasn't

sure he'd ever considered the position she was in, and where she'd be coming from, or what she brought from her past into her present.

"You are interested in me, right?" he asked.

She trilled out a laugh and stretched up on her toes to kiss his cheek. "Graham, I'm very interested in you." Her eyes twinkled now, but that determination loitered just beneath the surface. All of it faded into fear. "But I do need this to go slow, and I need you to understand that it might take time for me to come to certain...decisions."

"I can go slow," he said almost stupidly, the foolishness racing through him that he'd gotten his feelings hurt fast and furious. "And I guess now's a good time to say I don't like being called a beast. I'm not trying to be rude."

She had no idea what it was like, stepping into his father's shoes after an abrupt death, and trying to run a company he had no knowledge of and no inclination to head up. He'd worked non-stop for months to get his head wrapped around everything Springside Energy did, all while the general manager simply wanted him to go away.

And when that work was done for the day—which was laughable. The work at Springside was never really done— he had the entire lodge, the grounds, and the farm to take care of.

"What did I do?" he asked, drawing her into his arms and holding her against his chest. "To make you think I'm a bit of a beast?"

"It's just...it's just the way you say things," she said. "Like it doesn't sound like asking. It sounds like telling."

"I needed your help," he said. "I didn't mean to demand it."

"I know that."

"I'll work on it," he said.

"I have some things to work on too," she said. "But right now, I just want to hang these nameplates and then get the tree decorated." She stepped back and smiled at him, a cautious, beautiful smile. "Okay?"

"Okay." He swept one hand around her waist and brought her close again. "But I think maybe I need a kiss to make up for being called a beast behind my back." He smiled down at her, glad when she caught the teasing quality in his tone.

Her eyes drifted closed and she tipped her head back, an open invitation for him to kiss her. He took an extra moment to soak in her beauty, and then he claimed her mouth, this kiss just as wonderful, just as passionate, and just as life-changing as the first.

━━━━━

GRAHAM BROUGHT ANOTHER BOX OF ORNAMENTS IN FROM THE garage, the heat hitting him in the face. "This is it," he said as he set the glittering orbs on the floor in the foyer.

Laney exhaled and straightened, taking in the mess of boxes spread between the two of them. "I don't know if we can do this in a single day."

Bailey hummed to herself as she slipped another hook through the top of a red ball and hung it on one of the lowest branches. Graham let his eyes travel up the tree, realizing just how tall it was and big around it spanned, and how he probably shouldn't have left this task for the last day.

Or for himself.

His eyes met Laney's and locked, and she shrugged one shoulder in that classic Laney-way and said, "Maybe if we have chocolate...."

Graham grinned and turned back to the kitchen. A steaming pot of water sat on the stove and Celia slid a handful of lasagna noodles into it. "Celia," he said, listening to his own voice. Did he sound too demanding? He hadn't stomped in and yelled, "Hot chocolate in the next two minutes or you're fired!" That was something, right?

She turned toward him and scraped her bangs off her forehead. "Hey, Graham." She reminded him so much of his mother, and Graham was glad his mom had decided to stay at the lodge for the holidays. Then all the brothers could pamper her on this first year she was alone for the holidays.

She'd gone to Bora Bora for Thanksgiving, and Eli hadn't even served turkey or mashed potatoes.

"We're getting started on the tree decorating," he said, feeling like an idiot for how he was talking. This wasn't normal or who he was. "And Laney's wondering what the possibility of hot chocolate is?" He pitched his voice up on the last word as if it were a question.

Celia blinked at him, confusion on her face. "Graham?"

He was likewise confused. "Can you make us some hot chocolate while we decorate the tree?"

"Sure." She went over to the cupboard and pulled down three mugs. "I already have water heating."

"Thanks." He returned to the foyer and found Laney trying to hide her smile. "What?"

"Ah, there he is." She started laughing as she unwrapped another box of lights.

He rolled his eyes and growled, a very beastly thing to do, before bending to collect a box of red-and-white striped ornaments shaped like icicles. "All right, Bailey, hook me up with these."

The towhead came over, her bright blue eyes so out of place on a face that looked so much like Laney's. He didn't know her husband, but the man must've had blue eyes.

They worked together, the hot chocolate coming out only a few minutes later, and ornament by ornament, candy cane by candy cane, and Christmas song by Christmas song, the tree got decorated.

Graham groaned as he dismounted the ladder for what felt like the millionth time and stretched his back. Bailey had wandered into the kitchen at least an hour ago, and Celia had told Graham lunch was ready three times before she gave up.

Laney stood back, almost under the archway that led down the hall to his bedroom, her eyes raking from the top of the tree to the bottom. "I think it looks pretty good."

Graham caught her lingering on a spot near the top. "There's a bare patch up there." He looked at the mess on the floor, hating that he had to clean it all up. This deco-rating thing was entirely too much work. "Do we have anything else?"

"It's fine," Laney said. "We still have farm work to do."

He checked down the hall toward the garage before sweeping his arm around her waist. "It hasn't snowed nearly as much today. Should go faster."

She leaned into him a little bit, and he liked that she gave her exhaustion to him. He'd gladly shoulder it for her. "Let's get this cleaned up."

"How about you clean this up and I'll do the outside chores?"

Laney froze, her eyes now wide and glittering. "What?"

"I only have the three horses. I can get them done lickety-split and get down to your place before you even have half of this put away." He saw the indecision in her eyes and shrugged. "I mean, we can race."

He closed his eyes in a moment of idiocy. *We can race?* Were they four years old?

"Deal," she said. "I'll text you when I'm done, and if you're not done with your horses before I get all these put away, you...." She trailed off, and Graham wanted to bail her out but he also really wanted to know how she'd finish that sentence.

"I'll what?" he asked.

"Take me to dinner."

"I already asked you to dinner." He grinned at her and cocked one eyebrow.

"You're a beast." She pushed against his chest, a smile dancing in her eyes.

"Oh, you can't say that about everything." He laughed and added, "I get some time to get properly dressed for the outdoors." He gave her a quick kiss on the cheek and headed for the mudroom. "I'll yell at you when you can go."

He heard boxes sliding and plastic rustling, and he called, "Cheater!" as he shoved his feet into his boots. Laney giggled, the sound high and girlish and absolutely diving right into the soft places of his heart.

He thought about the word he'd called as he finished getting ready and burst out in the cold. *Cheater.*

Erica had cheated on him in Seattle, and he'd expected the sting, the shrinking of his chest, to linger with him forever. But it was gone. He tossed a last look at the back door of the lodge, wondering if Laney had anything to do with how healed his heart felt.

CHAPTER 11

L aney woke the next morning, the warmth in the lodge more comfortable than she'd been expecting. Maybe she had labeled Graham as a hairy beast who'd locked himself away in this giant house. But he did have a good heart, and everyone who met him seemed to love him, and she'd really enjoyed her time here.

But the snow was predicted to stop, and the power company had said they'd be out that afternoon to look at the lines, and he had a whole slew of people coming into town for the holidays.

You should go back to the ranch, she told herself as the night started to lighten to dawn. She obviously couldn't go until the electricity had been restored and the furnace had had a chance to get things toasty again.

So maybe another night, she thought, the idea grabbing on and holding tight. And if she was here tomorrow, she might as well stay all the way to Christmas Day.

A light knock sounded on the door and then Bailey's little voice said, "Mom? Are you awake?"

"Yep. Come in, bug."

The door opened and Bailey padded in wearing her pink nightgown, carrying her stuffed llama, and all three dogs trailing behind her. Laney didn't let her two animals on her bed, but apparently Barry and Clearwater had lost all civilization, because they jumped up on the bed and gave her looks like, *We can't believe we've been missing out on these soft mattresses all these years,* before turning and lying down.

Laney opened her arms and Bailey slid into bed with her. "What's up?"

"Something hit my window."

Laney glanced toward the window to her left but it was still too dark to see much. "Maybe it's windy."

"Clearwater barked."

"Clearwater barks if I sneeze."

Bailey snuggled in deeper, and Laney tucked the blanket around her and stroked her hair. "We're going to do the tree lighting today. You're excited about that, right?"

"Yeah."

"All of Graham's family is coming."

"I know. Celia said we're having chicken pot pie tonight."

Laney's mouth watered just thinking about it. She served chicken pot pie, but it was the frozen ones she simply put in the oven for an hour while she showered and twisted her wet hair into a bun, maybe ran the vacuum, and then took a ten-minute nap until the timer went off.

"We might not be here tonight," she said.

"Why not?" Bailey twisted her head to look up at her.

"When they get our power back on, we'll go back to the ranch."

"But you said Santa could bring the presents here."

"And he can. But if our house is fixed, we'll go back there."

Bailey frowned, but she settled back against Laney's side. "I think he might get confused with all the switching."

Laney didn't want to squash her daughter's dreams, but she didn't want to make her plans based on what a six-year-old believed about a mythical figure. "We'll see," she said, her standard answer when she didn't know what she was doing as a mother—which was all the time.

They settled into silence, and Laney did hear the wind whipping around outside, and she secretly hoped the power lines couldn't get repaired that afternoon. Then she wouldn't have to make a decision, and Bailey would be satisfied.

They dozed for a while, until the scent of coffee and something yeasty lifted into the air. Bailey rustled first, and when Laney opened her eyes, she found all three dogs waiting at the door. Clearwater whined, and Bailey got out of bed.

"I'll be right down, okay?" Laney asked.

"Okay." Bailey opened the door and let the dogs go through first. She left the door ajar and Laney heard her footsteps recede and then go down the steps. Laney wasn't particularly tired, but she sure did like lying in a warm bed for a few extra minutes.

When she finally got up and pulled on a gray sweater with a pair of jeans and went downstairs, she found everyone sitting at the dining room table, Belgian waffles mounded in front of them.

"There you are," Celia said, the way Laney's mother would have when she'd overslept. "I saved some bacon for you. These two were like wolves."

Graham lifted one shoulder in a non-apologetic shrug as his mouth was full of waffles and syrup.

"Oh, thank you," Laney said, not quite sure how to take being fussed over. It hadn't happened in so long, and her first instinct was to say, "I'm fine. I don't even like bacon," though the opposite was true.

She let Celia get the bacon from the oven and she loaded a Belgian waffle with strawberries and cream. "So," she said. "What's the plan for today?"

"Beau's helping me shuttle everyone from the airport," Graham said. "Farm chores this morning. Tree lighting at six."

"Dinner at six-fifteen," Celia said.

"Everyone will be here by four," Graham said. "I hope." He peered toward the windows down at the end of the table. "If the weather holds."

The sun shone outside, but Laney knew it held false warmth. She'd spent many winters in Wyoming, and she knew what the wind could do to noses and fingertips.

Breakfast ended, and she took a few extra minutes to

sip her coffee while Bailey helped Celia in the kitchen. Graham disappeared down the hall to his office with a look in Laney's direction, but she didn't follow him.

This reality felt a little too...easy. A little too good to be true. As soon as she got back to Echo Ridge Ranch, she'd be reminded of the stark truth of things. Not enough hours to do everything that needed to be done. Not enough money to go around.

But she did love Bailey, and Bailey loved her, the dogs, the horses, all of it. So Echo Ridge did have something this lodge didn't. Heart. Spirit. Love.

Sighing, Laney rinsed her dishes and put them in the dishwasher before saying, "Come on, Bailey. We have work to do."

———

As darkness fell, Laney tromped up the road to the lodge, which glowed with cheery yellow lights in the front windows. At the end of the drive, she took a moment to gaze at the building, which looked warm and welcoming and wonderful.

Everyone should've arrived this afternoon, and she wondered what kind of reception she'd get from the Whittaker brothers, their friends and other family members. Bailey had spent the morning working the ranch with her, but Laney had brought her back for lunch and gone back to the ranch to meet with the electric company alone.

A deep breath helped her center herself. Strengthen her resolve for what she needed to do. Her phone chimed as she took the first step down the cleared driveway, and she pulled it out to see Graham's name on the screen—and that she was late.

How close are you? his message read.

Two minutes, she typed out. *Coming down the drive now.*

A few seconds later, the front door opened, and a tall, broad-shouldered figure blocked the light spilling out. Laney's breath caught and she couldn't even see the man. She couldn't help feeling nervous to meet his whole family and spend Christmas with them, but she also knew some of the butterflies were simply because she hadn't yet kissed Graham that day and she wanted to.

He met her at the sidewalk, his leather jacket not nearly bulky enough to stave off the cold. His breath puffed out as he smiled. "Hey, pretty lady."

Laney's grin popped onto her face and she paused to lean into his warmth. "Hey."

"How'd it go down there?"

She exhaled, sending her own cloud of white into the chilly air. "Not great. The lines are severed, and require a full crew."

His arms came around her, holding her close to his heartbeat, enveloping her in the scent of his skin, his clothes, him. He smelled like cotton, and air freshener, and soap, and something woodsy. "How soon can they get a whole crew out?"

"They won't have a full crew until after the new year." She spoke with measured syllables, hoping he'd hear the desperation in her voice. "Hey, it saves me on heat, right?" She tried a chuckle, but it didn't quite come out right.

"So you'll stay with me until then." The way he said it, like it would just be so, actually warmed Laney this time.

"If we can," she said. "I can pay for the room."

"Don't be ridiculous."

"People used to pay for those rooms, you know."

"I know." He laced his fingers through hers and faced the house. "You ready for this?" That was all. No negotiation. She simply would not be paying rent.

"How crazy is it?"

"Compared to living alone? A nightmare." He chuckled. "But it actually feels kinda nice to have everyone here too."

She squeezed his hand. "All right, cowboy. Let's do this."

But he didn't move. "I just...." He gazed down at her, and Laney lost herself in the darkness of his eyes, the emotion streaming from them. "I'm wondering how I introduce you."

Because she wanted to, she tipped up onto her toes and skated her lips across his. He quickly caught her waist and drew her close again, kissing her more firmly the second time.

"So girlfriend should work," Laney whispered against his lips, kissing him one more time and hoping the term didn't shock him—or his family—too much.

"Not best friend?" he asked.

"I think I can be both." She put a couple of inches between them and searched his face. "Don't you?"

"I've never thought about it."

"You weren't friends with any of your girlfriends?"

"Well, yeah, I mean...I guess."

"I was best friends with my husband." Laney gazed back at the house. "Once upon a time." She didn't want to go down that road, not at Christmas. Thinking of Mike would only make her angry, and she didn't want to spend another holiday furious. She'd checked the house for mail, and when she didn't find any, she'd called the post office.

No packages. No gifts.

Bailey's father had forgotten her—again.

She drew in a breath and forced the thoughts out with mere oxygen. "I have presents at my house," she said. "Maybe you could help me get them tomorrow, sneak them up here to the lodge?"

"Of course." He kneaded her closer, held her for another moment.

Someone opened the front door and called, "Graham? We're ready in here."

He chuckled and said, "That'll be Eli. Always keeping us on schedule." He walked toward the house, Laney's hand securely in his, muttering, "Girlfriend. Hey, guys, you remember Laney Boyd? She's my girlfriend," to himself.

Laney grinned at the ground, liking the way the word sounded coming out of his mouth, the way she'd long suspected she would. Now, if she could just get through meeting everyone, she could maybe take a decent breath and enjoy the festivities.

CHAPTER 12

G raham stopped just short of opening the front door. "What about Bailey?" So maybe he had some nerves about announcing to his whole family at the same time that he'd gone and gotten himself a girlfriend in the past three days. He could see their faces now; his mother's eyes full of surprise, Andrew's squinted gaze as he tried to figure out if Graham was kidding or not....

"We've talked about me dating again," she said.

"She's six."

"She's not stupid." Laney looked up at him, her light green eyes blazing with a strange sort of fire.

"Look who's being beastly now." Graham cracked a smile but his chest did sting the tiniest bit. He just felt so out of his element with a new relationship, especially since Laney's situation wasn't easy and came with a six-year-old. Graham had no idea how to relate to children, though he thought he got along just fine with Bailey.

She sighed and said, "She started first grade this year. She knows other people have dads. There was a 'Bring Your Dad to School Day,' and Bailey and I talked a lot about her dad, and where he was, and that I might find someone else to...." She trailed off, and though it was dark, Graham could definitely see the hint of a blush there.

"Marry?" He forced the word out of his mouth. Best friend or boyfriend was certainly more palatable, as Graham had never really envisioned himself as a husband and father.

"I mean, not right now." Laney squeezed his hand. "You look like you're going to throw up." She tacked a giggle onto the end of her sentence, but she wasn't far off.

"I'm just—" He cleared his throat. "It's a lot to take in on short notice."

"So maybe just start with *we're starting to see each other*. I mean, we haven't even been to dinner yet."

They were practically living together—and would be for at least another week. But he squared his shoulders, a bit of the sound inside leaking through the solid wood door. "Okay." He opened the door before she could say anything and gripped her hand as he stepped inside.

"There he is." Eli stood nearest to the door, his tie a bit looser than before. Just the fact that he traveled in a white shirt and tie said a lot about the second youngest brother, but Graham liked Eli the best.

He was down-to-earth and practical. He had lighter brown hair than Graham, but the same glinting, dark chocolate-colored eyes.

"Eli," Graham said. "You remember Laney Boyd, don't you?"

It was as if the conversation had been muted. Even the Christmas music that Celia had started through the overhead speakers hit a lull, making the silence the only thing between him and everyone else.

Eli's appraising eyes ran down the length of Laney's body and back to her face. It only took a second, maybe two, but Graham felt like it had taken an hour, and his brother definitely saw their joined hands.

"Laney Boyd." He stepped forward and gave her a quick side-hug. "Of course."

"It's McAllister now," she said with a smile. "You're looking great, Eli."

He twisted back to the foyer, which was filled with people, and said, "Thanks. Come meet my son. He was thrilled to see your daughter here. Stockton, where are you?"

Graham's nephew emerged from behind the tree, a portable game machine in his hand. He passed it to his father when he arrived and looked up at them. "Uncle Graham, this place is awesome."

"Thanks, bud." Graham grinned at the boy, hoping he'd get to see him a lot while Eli was here. Bora Bora was too far away. "This is my girlfriend, Laney. It's her daughter Bailey you're playing with."

Stockton, ever the gentleman, stuck out his hand. "Nice to meet you."

"Oh, well." Laney giggled and shook the child's hand. "Nice to meet you too." She released Graham's hand and bent down to the boy's level. "If you find me later, I'll make sure you know where your uncle keeps the treats."

Stockton's eyes rounded and he grinned. "All right."

"Did I hear right?" Graham's mother arrived on the scene and put a protective arm around Stockton. "You two are dating?"

Graham exchanged a look with Laney, but she simply smiled at him, her face the most beautiful thing he'd ever seen. "Kind of, Mom."

"Kind of?" Andrew demanded. He, at least, wore a pair of jeans, a blue T-shirt, and a gray hoodie.

"I've asked her out." Graham straightened, trying to gain the half-inch of height he had over his brother. "But with the storms, we haven't made it out of the lodge yet."

"Come meet my friends." Eli guided Laney and Stockton away from Graham, and he watched his girl-friend go, her long hair swaying as she walked over to two men and a woman—Eli's friends and nanny. Beau joined the circle of people surrounding Graham, and he had no choice but to stay.

Celia caught his eye from her position against the wall leading into the hall, a small smile on her face. Graham felt his neck heat, but he knew he had her approval.

"Graham, I didn't know you and Laney were even that close." Beau sipped from a bottle of water, his question-that-wasn't-really-a-question so much like a lawyer it was annoying.

"Of course we are," Graham said. "She's the closest neighbor I have out here, and she's been helping me with the farm for a year."

"You've never mentioned her before." His mother wore a look of concern like maybe Laney had bewitched him somehow.

Honestly, Graham could barely think straight. "I'm mentioning her now." He glanced past Andrew to where Laney laughed at something Meg, the nanny, had said.

"Look, it's new, okay? She's been staying here for a couple of days because the power lines at her place are down. She'll be here through the holidays, and I like her." He practically hissed the last couple of words as Bailey skipped over.

"Graham, remember how you said I could pass out the Christmas Eve gifts?"

He swept his gaze past the members of his family and focused on the little girl. "'Course I do, Bay. Are you ready? We'll do them right after the lighting."

"Stockton wants to help."

"Oh, well, I think that's okay. Don't you?"

She looked torn, but she glanced over her shoulder to where Stockton stood with his nanny and back to Graham. "Yeah, it's okay."

"Okay, well, go get them from Celia, and I'll get everyone ready for the lighting." Because then the conversation with his mother and brothers would be over. Bailey skipped away, and he said, "All right, everyone. I think we're ready to do the tree lighting. I'm told it's best if you stand over here." He indicated the fireplace, which had a dozen stockings hung along its length and waited while everyone came over.

He claimed Laney's hand again as soon as she came

within arm's reach, his anxiety teeming near the top of his control. "Are we ready?" The evergreen sat in darkness, though the ornaments glinted from the overhead lights.

"No," Bailey said. "Get that light behind you, Mom."

Laney twisted and switched off the porch light while Celia flipped off the lights in the kitchen and hallway.

"Now we're ready," the six-year-old announced. "Go ahead Graham."

He grinned and while he hadn't been planning a speech, he stepped out of the crowd and stood in front of them. "I'm so glad we're all here together this Christmas." His emotions skyrocketed, and the fact that his father wasn't there stuck in his throat.

Several long seconds passed before he was able to continue, and he caught his mother wiping her eyes. "Dad loved the holidays, and he'd always give us a small gift on Christmas Eve. So we'll be doing that right after this, and then Celia has dinner in the kitchen." He surveyed the group, finding his love for each of them—even those he didn't know well and had only met that afternoon —growing.

"I thank God you could all travel here safely to be with us, and Andrew will say grace over the food once we're in the dining room." He wasn't particularly long-winded, and he felt emotionally spent standing in front of them all. "Anyone have anything else they want to say? Mom?"

She shook her head, a sniffle the only sound. "You did great, Graham."

He stepped back into his place. "All right then. I'll turn on the lights." He picked up the remote that controlled the outlet where he'd plugged in the tree and pushed a button. The white lights burst to life, illuminating the silver, red, green, blue, and gold bulbs and casting a magical glow on the entire room.

Everyone ooh'ed and ahh'ed, and Laney leaned into him and sighed. "It's beautiful."

The tree was beautiful, but all Graham could see was the work he and Bailey and Laney had spent on it. And he was glad he hadn't passed the task onto someone else. That was time he'd spent with them that no one could take from him.

He pressed a kiss to the top of her head, and said, "I'm glad you're here." And while he'd invited her ages ago, he wondered if her power hadn't gone out if they'd really be standing where they were.

Thank you, he sent heavenward, more grateful for downed power lines in this moment than any other time.

"Presents!" Bailey announced, and she lunged for the tree, where she'd helped him arrange the gifts that morning.

Graham kept a tight grip on Laney's hand as the presents were handed out. They weren't anything special, but his father had taught him not to downplay a gift. It could be exactly what someone needed.

"Socks," Andrew announced after he'd ripped open his package. "These are nice, Graham." He beamed at his brother. "Thanks."

Everyone got socks, and not a single person acted like they didn't want them. Graham basked in the homey feeling permeating the huge foyer, and he saw Meg help

Stockton replace his socks with the new ones he'd just gotten. The child came prancing over.

"Look, Uncle Graham!" He held up one foot. "Mine have reindeers on them." He looked like he'd just been given the world, and Graham scooped him up and said, "They sure do, bud. Let's go eat."

Graham waved his hand above his head as he side-stepped the mess and navigated past the tree. "Time to eat. Follow me."

Everyone did, and he pointed out the place settings Bailey had made that afternoon while Laney had been down at the ranch with the power company. "Find your name. No switcheroos. Lots of planning went into the seating arrangements."

He placed Stockton on his chair and said, "I'm right next to you, bud." But Graham didn't sit right away. He waited until Laney entered the dining room and then he pulled out her chair for her, as she'd been assigned to his right side.

Bailey already sat next to her, a look of pure delight on her face. Once everyone had taken their seats, Graham said, "Andrew, if you're ready."

His brother stood and cleared his throat. In his strong, deep voice, he started, "Lord, we thank Thee for this day, for bringing us all here safely to celebrate the season of Thy birth...."

Graham lost himself in the peacefulness of the moment, the silence of sacredness that accompanied the brief moment after Andrew said "Amen," and everyone echoed him before the clatter of silverware on plates began and chatter about travel, jobs, and life began.

He took one extra moment with his fork in his hand to bask in the energy in this lodge, and he wanted to have it available to him more often.

"You okay?" Laney touched his leg under the table, and Graham pulled himself out of his introspection.

"Yeah." He looked at her. "Yes." He reached for the chicken pot pie and dished himself some, then took the salad bowl from her. "You?"

"Best I've been in a while." She beamed at him and then turned to help Bailey with her food.

And Graham felt sure those words would keep him warm though the long winter ahead.

CHAPTER 13

L aney had never had such a magical Christmas. Santa managed to find them, and she managed to kiss Graham under the mistletoe one of Eli's friends had hung at the bottom of the stairs leading into the basement, and it was wonderful having meals provided for her. Hot water in her private bathroom. A warm, comfortable bed she didn't have to make in the morning if she didn't want to.

But after that kiss on Christmas morning, she'd had a very hard time getting Graham alone. He was always surrounded by his brothers, talking and laughing. Laney learned that the four of them hadn't been together since their father's funeral, and she hadn't wanted to impose on their family reunion.

So more often than not, she found herself hanging out with Meg and the kids. On Christmas Day, when everyone had drifted to quiet spots to take naps, she wandered into

Bailey's room. All three dogs looked up, but no one came to greet her.

"Bay? Can I talk to you for a second?"

Bailey set down her tablet and said, "Okay."

"It's about me and Graham." She perched on the edge of the bed, praying for six-year-old words to explain an adult situation. "You like Graham, right?"

"Yeah." She blinked. "You like Graham too."

"Right." Laney smiled at her hands which lay in her lap. "I like Graham too. The kind of like where you hold hands and kiss and stuff." Her heart did a jig in her chest. "It's nothing too serious yet. We haven't even gone out."

"But you will go out with him."

"Probably, Bay, yes."

"So I'll get to go to Grandma's." She reached over and patted Barry's head, which caused the dog to stretch out and groan.

Laney chuckled. "Yes, Bailey, most likely. When I go out with Graham, you'll stay with Grandma so I can go alone."

"You told me not to be alone with boys."

"Right." She tapped Bailey on the nose. "Because you're a kid. When you're an adult, you can make a decision for when's a good time to be alone with a boy and when it's not a good idea."

"I think you can be alone with Graham. He seems nice."

Laney smiled at Bailey. "He does seem that way, doesn't he?" Bailey didn't get the joke, and Laney stood. "Okay, go back to your 'resting'. I'm going to go lie down too." She went next door to her room, but she didn't feel sleepy. She felt caged. Alone. Trapped all by herself, and while she was glad she'd been able to talk to Bailey, she didn't like lying around without anything to do.

Perhaps Celia would have something for her to do in the kitchen, but when Laney went down there, she found the main level of the house completely deserted. A cheer came up the steps from the basement, and she faced the doorway as she contemplated going down to see what all the fuss was.

But she hadn't been invited, and she thought it was quiet time for a while anyway. So she went back upstairs and into her room, wishing her text to Graham didn't go unanswered.

————

By the time two more days had passed, the restlessness in her muscles—her very soul—drove her out of the lodge and down to Echo Ridge Ranch. She told only Bailey where she was going and her daughter had promised to stay out of trouble and inside the lodge.

"Hey, Starlight." Laney approached the horse that had helped her through some of the most trying times of her life. When Mike had left. When Laney had packed up everything he'd left behind and taken it to good will. When she'd filed for divorce.

The black mare had always been there, just like now. She nickered, and Laney leaned into her palm against the horse's nose. "I don't know." She wanted to believe that Graham wouldn't abandon her and Bailey the way Mike had. She also wanted to believe their five-day relationship hadn't been a fluke or some sort of fling. That he was simply preoccupied with his family.

"But what else will he become preoccupied with?" she asked the horse. Starlight closed her eyes and opened them again, nothing else to say apparently.

Laney spent another few minutes with the horse and then got to work. After all, all the animals needed to be fed, and Laney needed more clothes if she and Bailey were going to stay at the lodge for another five days.

Because they'd moved the chickens into the barn, she found the beasts clucking happily in their nests. Laney worked methodically, slowly even, and got all the chores done. With no housework to do, a few hours of her day had been cleared up.

She faced the lodge, thinking of the little house on the very edge of her property. After running inside and throwing a few more sets of clean clothes into a bag, she set off for the cabin on the fence line. The trek through the snow left her tired and wet, but when the little round building without a back door came into view, her heart lifted.

She'd built this place with her father, and it was one of her strongest childhood memories. She'd barely been able to keep up with him as he hauled lumber and hammered nails, but she'd loved the look of him in his cowboy hat and tool belt.

She'd handed him tools, brought him food and water, and spent hours listening to him talk about their land, the ranch, and how much he loved it. By the time she was nine years old, she loved Echo Ridge as much as he did. And since she didn't have any brothers to work the ranch, Laney had learned all the chores by age twelve.

Gentry, her younger sister, didn't want anything to do with horses or hay, and that had been just fine with Laney. She'd just inherited the ranch a little too soon, as her father was taken home to heaven much too young.

She sighed and went around to the front door, which had a few feet of snow blown against it. She brushed the offending substance away from the door jamb and kicked as much back as she could. When she finally got in, she automatically stretched for the light switch and flipped it.

The lights came on.

This place had electricity.

A buzz tiptoed down her arms and along her shoulders, zinging up into her hair. She and Bailey could stay here. Though the place was small, there were two bedrooms, running water, a kitchen. She'd stockpiled several days' worth of firewood in the lean-to off the front porch, and she and Bailey could survive just fine here.

Her thoughts tumbled. Part of her really wanted her privacy back, though no one pressed her to spend meals with them, or get up earlier than she wanted. She was well-fed at the lodge, but her heart pinched.

She was lonely there.

Bailey had found a new playmate, and Meg's every breath was dedicated to making sure Stockton was happy. Laney had no role at the lodge, and Graham didn't seem to have time for her.

She'd been abandoned once before. She wouldn't put

herself or Bailey through that again. And as soon as she and Bailey left the lodge, it would probably be a miracle if they saw Graham once a week.

After all, the man worked non-stop, even during Christmastime.

Laney turned off the light, wishing her thoughts would darken just as easily. They didn't, and she moved over to the couch and collapsed onto it. Melting snow permeated her boots and socks, and she wanted nothing more than to take a hot bath.

So she did, Graham never far from the center of her thoughts.

———

SHE SERIOUSLY CONSIDERED STAYING AT THE CABIN FOR THE night, but she couldn't leave Bailey up at the lodge without supervision. She wouldn't ask Graham for his permission, so after she'd dried her hair and knotted it under her knit cap, she started up the hill toward the lodge.

She'd stayed in the hot water longer than she should've, because darkness had dunked the day into nothing more than shadows and there was no trail to follow. She kept one eye on the light lifting into the air just over the hill and kept her feet moving in the right direction.

The house finally came into view, just beyond Graham's outbuildings. The path became easier, and she wondered if he had heated sidewalks his were so clear.

Pausing, she drank in the sight of the lodge, with several of the back windows lit from within. It was the perfect country retreat, and she felt a measure of gratitude that she'd been allowed a few days at Whiskey Mountain Lodge.

She burst into the mudroom to a wall of warmth, thank goodness. Though she'd just had a bath, a chill had seeped into her very bones on the trek here from the cabin. Boot-steps sounded—angry bootsteps—and Graham appeared from the kitchen.

"There you are." He didn't seem happy about it.

"Here I am." She shrugged out of her coat, glad when Graham stepped forward to help her with one offending sleeve that wouldn't slide down.

"I've been worried about you." He spoke in a low voice and edged even tighter into her personal space.

"I'm fine." She bent to untie her boots.

"I didn't ask if you were okay."

She finally got the courage to look into his eyes. A storm swirled in his, and she couldn't tell if it was fueled by frustration or desire. His hand came up and drifted down the side of her face, barely touching her and yet branding her all the same.

"You never answered any of my texts."

"I didn't get any." She swallowed, the words about the electricity at the cabin springing to the back of her throat.

"Where were you?"

"The ranch."

"You get my texts down there." He tilted his head,

clearly trying to hear or see something she hadn't said or showed him. "Laney?"

She wanted to spill her guts to him. Pour out her loneliness and ask him to spend time with her while she was here. Selfishness pulled through her before she could say anything too damaging, and she cleared her throat.

"I went out walking." She indicated the wet bottoms of her jeans, where water had seeped almost all the way to her knees. "Maybe I lost reception." As if proving her point, her cell phone chimed three, four, five, six times in rapid succession. She pulled it out of her pocket and looked at the messages. "Here they are now."

She flashed the phone in his direction but he didn't even glance at it. "Laney, I can tell something's different."

Looking into his eyes, her entire past flashed through her mind. Had she said enough to Mike before he left? If she'd tried harder, would he have stayed?

"I feel left out," she blurted without giving herself a chance to censor her words. "Your family is here, and I get this is a special time for you, and...." She exhaled and pulled her hat off. She unknotted her hair and let it fall over her shoulders. "I'm not trying to be selfish, but I feel...I'm lonely. Even here, with all of you. I don't fit."

"Of course you do." Graham gathered her into his arms, and she definitely fit there. She took a deep drag of his T-shirt, which held the scent of his cologne and his fabric softener.

"I don't want to be left behind," she said so quietly she wasn't sure he'd heard her. She pushed away from him and strengthened her resolve. "I've lived through a man leaving me for something he deemed better, and I won't do it again. I won't allow Bailey to go through that."

Graham blinked at her, the confusion racing through his eyes somewhat comforting. "I'm not abandoning anything. I live here." He gestured back toward the kitchen. "My brothers and I have been talking about making this lodge into what it was meant to be. Andrew has degrees and experience in marketing and public relations. Eli runs the biggest resort in Bora Bora. Beau already handles all the legalities for Springside Energy, and he said he'd look into what we have to do to make this place a legal lodge again."

Laney had no idea why he was telling her this, but she couldn't help feeling a twinge of guilt at the relationships he had with his brothers. Gentry hadn't sent a card or gift this Christmas either, though Laney continued to send small things to her for her birthday and other special events. Her sister was off living in California or New York. Laney wasn't exactly sure.

"That's great," she said, trying to make her voice light. But Graham was as smart as he was handsome, and he heard the forced measure of nonchalance in her tone.

"I'm just saying I'm not going anywhere."

"Okay."

"Okay." He backed up another step, and Laney hated the distance—physical and emotional—between them. "Are you going to read those texts?" He indicated her phone, and she looked at it.

Bailey said you went down to the ranch. Wondering if you wanted to go to dinner tonight.

Meg said she can watch Bailey, no problem.

I mean, it's fine if you don't want to.

Laney? Are you all right? I'm worried I haven't heard back from you.

So I guess we won't go to dinner tonight.

She raised her eyes to his. "I didn't get these."

His voice softened, along with the dangerous edge in his eyes. "I know. I heard your phone chime."

"Is it too late for dinner?" Because she really wanted to go, and she was starving. Of course, the aroma coming from the kitchen meant Celia had been at work and would most like have something as restaurant-worthy as anything in Coral Canyon.

"I haven't eaten yet."

"Can I have ten minutes to change?"

Graham regarded her for a moment, those beautiful eyes taking on a sparkle. "A beast would insist we go now because it's already going to be busy. But you know what? Take fifteen minutes."

Laney burst into laughter, glad when Graham joined her. She gave him a quick hug, swept her lips across his stubbled jaw, and ran upstairs to change for her first date with Graham Whittaker.

CHAPTER 14

Graham paced in his office, Laney's words haunting him. *I've lived through a man leaving me for something he deemed better, and I won't do it again. I won't allow Bailey to go through that.*

They hadn't even gone out yet, and she was thinking marriage—she'd said not right away, but he wasn't stupid. Laney didn't do anything halfway, he knew that much about her. And now she was fretting about him abandoning her and Bailey—and they *hadn't even gone out yet.*

He exhaled, the pressure from this date already near peak levels, and ran his hand down the side of his face, picked up his cowboy hat, and positioned in over his too-long hair. "You want to go out with her," he told himself. When she hadn't answered that afternoon, his anger had taken on a life of its own.

He'd left everyone to do whatever they wanted, and he'd gotten through a list of emails and a pile of forms for payroll. Eli had come in and started talking about making the lodge a summer and winter destination, and Graham liked the idea.

He liked the idea of Andrew moving back to Coral Canyon and becoming the lodge's marketing expert. He wanted Eli and Stockton to stay in town too. Throughout the past year, Graham had been terribly isolated, and he hadn't even known it.

Sure, he could buy whatever he wanted, but he couldn't buy friendship, brotherhood, family love. Somehow, his brothers had felt the same things he had over the past few days, and as the new year approached, Graham finally felt like maybe it would be worth living through. Embracing. Enjoying.

And when he pictured the next twelve months and the changes they brought, Laney was at his side. So maybe she was thinking really far down the road. He couldn't blame her for that, could he? She had a daughter to consider, and a past to unpack.

"Hey."

He turned toward the sound of her voice, relief washing through him at the simple sight of her. Yes, he could give her the reassurance that he wouldn't abandon her. He wouldn't even know where to go, because leaving Coral Canyon wasn't an option.

"You working?"

"A little, earlier." He approached her. "I just want to ask you something before we go."

Her eyes met his, and he almost lost the words. "Yeah?"

"You're beautiful."

She ducked her head as a smile touched her lips. "That's not a question."

Graham ran his fingertips up her forearm, glad when goose bumps broke out on her skin. At least he wasn't the only one invested in the relationship. "I wanted to ask you to separate me from your ex."

Those eyes sprang back to his, and now they held fire. "I haven't—"

"You have," he said gently, sweeping both hands up her arms to her shoulders and back to her hands, where he laced her fingers between his. "And I don't blame you. But I'm not Mike McAllister, just like you're not my cheating ex-girlfriend from Seattle." He hadn't meant to say that last bit, but it was out now, and the flames in Laney's eyes went out.

"She cheated on you?"

"At least three times, with three different guys." His voice hardly sounded like his. "So when my dad died, it was really easy to leave my life in Seattle. Well." He shrugged and gave a dark chuckle. "Nothing was easy about returning to Coral Canyon, but I didn't want to stay in Seattle, so there was that."

"I'm so sorry. I didn't know."

"That's because I've been a beastly best friend," he said. "Always calling you for help but not really *talking* to you."

"You're a great best friend," she said. "You always have been. You know when to ask me stuff and when to let me be. I've always liked that about you."

"Oh yeah?" His gaze dropped to her mouth, and she'd put something shiny and pink on her lips.

"Yeah." She eased into his arms, a coy smile sending his pulse to the back of his throat.

"I like you, Laney McAllister," he said just before claiming her mouth with his. She kissed him back as if she liked him too, and Graham definitely wanted the next year to include a lot of Laney.

Forty-five minutes later, he sat across from her at The Devil's Tower, the only restaurant worth sitting down to eat, in Graham's opinion. Coral Canyon had a lot of fast casual places, with drive-through windows so he could take his burrito or burger or pizza home and eat it.

But The Devil's Tower was an experience, from the alien-like music to the menu. They only served towers of things—onion rings, sliders, grilled cheese sandwiches, even their salads were stacked and served vertically.

He loved the barbecue slider tower and the Tower of Power—a stack of mini-burgers layered with tomato, avocado, onion crisps, and bacon.

"Have you been here?" he asked.

"Of course," she said. "I didn't just move back last year."

"When did you move back?" He studied the menu like he needed to find something to order. But he knew he'd take the fried cheese pillar as an appetizer and the Tower of Power for his meal. And probably a French fry skyscraper too.

"Oh, about five years ago." Laney gave him a tight smile. "My dad died, and Mom didn't love ranching the way I do. I came back with Bailey for about eight months while my husband finished school. Then he joined us."

"You said he didn't stay long." Graham put his menu down, interested in this part of her past.

"Only nine months. He wasn't cut out for ranch life either." She studied him like maybe she'd be able to find the gene that indicated a person was into ranching just by looking. "You seem to like your horses."

"Sure," he said. "I wouldn't call myself a rancher. But then again, I wasn't interested in running Springside Energy either, and I'm doing that."

"Doing it well, I've heard."

Graham ran his fingers along his beard, thinking about what she'd said. "I don't know about that. According to Dwight, I'm probably screwing everything up."

"Dwight Rogers?" Laney laughed. "He only knew what your dad told him."

Graham put a smile on his face, though he rarely wore one when thinking about or dealing with Dwight. "Yes, well, things change, and my dad's not here anymore."

Laney sobered, and Graham hated that he'd put a damper on the conversation before they'd even ordered. "It gets a little easier," she finally said, sliding her hand across the table and layering it over his. "My dad's been gone about five years now, and it's just a little pinch behind my heart these days."

Graham nodded, because his emotions felt more like a cyclone than a pinch. The missing, the anger, the loneliness, the desperation all swirled together in perfect harmony, and he couldn't speak.

"So the cabin has power," Laney said, which made Graham focus on something else. "I'm thinking about taking Bailey and moving down there."

"You don't need to do that." He practically barked the words at her, and he leaned back in the booth, sliding his hand out from under hers.

The waitress appeared at that moment, and Graham took the excuse to order drinks and appetizers. As soon as Sylvia had left though, Laney said, "Your place is nearly full."

"It's fine," he said. "I...." Could he say the thoughts of his heart? What if Laney found them too forward? Read too much into them?

"I like having you there," he said, pushing himself to be brave, something he'd had to do a lot this past year. "I feel like if you go back to your ranch—or even the cabin—I won't...I'll...."

"Forget about me?"

"No," he said quickly, trying to find the right explanation. "But we won't get to spend as much time together, and I won't get to know you as quickly as I'd like." There. That didn't sound too needy. Or like he had to have her nearby to even think about her. If she knew how often she played the starring role in his thoughts, he'd be embarrassed.

She tucked her hair behind her ear, his answer apparently satisfactory. "I'm not sure I could pull Bailey away at this point."

"Then you'll stay."

"I guess so."

"Don't say it with so much enthusiasm," he teased.

She laughed, and Graham did too, and when their eyes met again, Graham felt himself slipping a little bit. He'd fallen like this before—once—and he knew where he'd end up if he allowed himself to keep pursuing this relationship.

With a wedding band on his finger and a wife in his life.

And while he'd thought he didn't need or want those things, if they came with Laney, he suddenly did want them. Very much.

"So," she said. "Tell me what you do at work."

He groaned, but he started talking about the robot he'd been developing for the past eight months that could potentially change how the entire business of fracking worked. To her credit, Laney acted interested, and that further endeared her to Graham.

That, and she ate an entire skyscraper of French fries by herself.

———

GRAHAM POINTED TO SOMETHING ON ONE OF THE PAPERS IN front of Eli. "But if I moved downstairs, we could rent out these three rooms too."

"If we're really thinking about renting out the rooms, you need an on-site staff." Eli pulled out another booklet. "This is the staff directory at Pure Paradise." He dropped it on top of the other folders and lists the brothers had been working on and discussing for days.

"Yeah, but they're at least a hundred times bigger than

this." Andrew leaned forward. "We've got six bedrooms upstairs. That's nine hundred dollars a night if we sell them for one-fifty, which I think we've decided on." He glanced at Graham and then Eli. Beau hadn't arrived from the valley yet, but he wasn't going to be too involved in the start up of Whiskey Mountain Lodge.

Graham waved for Andrew to go on. "So we need, maximum, someone to clean six rooms a day. How long can that take?"

"Thirty minutes per room, tops," Eli said. "Or we get someone else."

"This isn't a luxury resort on the beach," Graham said. "But it's definitely not full time."

"So that person can help in the kitchen," Andrew said. "And if we're going to serve dinner every night, we'll need someone here in the afternoons doing that."

"So someone to clean in the mornings, and someone to cook in the afternoons. That's full time work." Graham made a note on his phone. "And I have Celia already. What if she wants to be the cook but not the housekeeper?"

"You have a housekeeper too."

"And we think we want to offer Celia and Annie a place to live here?" Graham hadn't included that in his offer to them, but they were both part-time. Neither seemed to mind the hours he gave them.

"I don't know," Eli said. "Do we?"

"I don't think we need full-time on-site staff if we're all going to live here too." Andrew leaned back in his chair.

Surprise pulled through Graham. "You guys are moving in too?"

"The basement is empty," Andrew said. "And we're all single."

Single. The word rang in Graham's head. "Well, things change."

"Oh, right." Eli chuckled. "Because you're dating Laney now."

"She doesn't do things lightly," Graham said, determining that would be the last thing he'd say about her or their relationship.

"So let's say you get married." Andrew waved his hand toward Graham and then Eli, who nodded in acknowledgement. "Your master bedroom is like a small apartment. And Bailey could have the room right across the hall." He gestured again, and Graham smiled at the way his brother couldn't seem to say a sentence without his hands.

"They'd still have use of the kitchen. There are private living areas in the basement, your office, the small TV room across from the mudroom." Andrew started nodding. "The main festivities for the lodge guests would be in the foyer, which is big enough for movie nights, tree lightings, popcorn tastings, whatever else we want to do."

"And it's more than they'd get at a hotel," Eli tossed in. "And I'll get the boarding stable up and running, and we'll have a pool in the back in the summer, and easy access to hiking trails, a private entrance to the National Park...." He lifted his eyebrows as if to say *Enough said.*

Graham didn't know what to say. The idea of having

strangers living upstairs didn't sit very straight in his gut. But he wanted his brothers to come back to Coral Canyon. He'd seen his mother's face with all of her sons here, and if he could get Andrew and Eli back in town, he'd do it.

Both of his brothers watched him, waiting. "Let's get Beau on the documentation we need to be a legally operating lodge," he said, and Andrew cheered.

He immediately turned to Eli and said, "I get the gray room downstairs."

Eli rolled his eyes. "Fine. I'll take the blue one. And Stockton can have the one beside me."

"What about when you guys get married?" Graham asked.

Eli blinked at him and then started laughing. "Oh, brother," he said as he stood, their meeting clearly over. "I'm never doing that again." He headed for the door, and Andrew stood to follow him.

"Yeah, I'm with Eli," Andrew said. "Except I've never been married, so I can't say again."

Graham waited until his brothers left him alone in the office and then he muttered, "Yeah, that's what I thought, but look at me now." He reached for his phone so he could talk to Laney, the one person he wanted to share everything with.

CHAPTER 15

L aney hummed to herself as she packed the clothes she'd brought with her to the lodge. The power had been restored at the ranch yesterday, and she and Bailey were returning tomorrow, New Year's Day.

Graham had been *very* convincing when he'd asked her to stay for the New Year's Eve party that night. Whispers about kissing under a disco ball had entered her ears, and she'd finally admitted that he could recite a shopping list in that husky voice of his and she'd probably melt into him and agree to whatever he'd said, the way she had that morning.

But since she'd come to Whiskey Mountain Lodge a few days before Christmas and had been here so long, she had way more than she could fit in the bag she had. So she'd be making a couple of trips today to get most of her and Bailey's stuff back home.

"Where we belong," she murmured as she folded

another sweater. She liked being so close to Graham, but sometimes distance helped a relationship. It definitely would help Laney get some of her crooked thoughts straightened out.

"Knock, knock."

She jumped at the sound of Graham's voice outside her bedroom. To her knowledge, he never came upstairs.

"Hey." She tossed the shirt she'd just picked up to the bed and moved in front of the pile of laundry. "What're you...what're you doing up here?"

"Seeing if you wanted to grab lunch before taking a load back to your place." He flashed that sexy smile that made her want to throw herself into his arms and kiss that mouth until it wasn't grinning quite so coyly.

"Yeah, sure."

"I'm ready whenever you are."

Of course he was. He seemed to do whatever he wanted, whenever he wanted. She'd been impressed by his work ethic, because by the time he emerged from his office in the morning, he already looked like he'd been up for hours. He got all the chores done around the farm, and he'd been meeting with his brothers behind closed doors too.

He'd told her a lot about it, and she hoped he and his brothers were successful at making Whiskey Mountain Lodge into what they wanted it to be.

She handed him her stuffed bag and said, "Use your muscles for this, cowboy."

He chuckled as he took it, sweeping his free arm around her waist and pinning her against his body before

HER COWBOY BILLIONAIRE BEST FRIEND 157

he kissed her. This kiss was slow, sensual, exploratory. She let him take his time, her heartbeat accelerating with each moment that passed.

When he kissed her like this, she'd learned that he was feeling vulnerable and needed some sort of reassurance. So she returned his affection with as much passion as he gave her.

"Ready now," he finally whispered. When he stepped back, he looked at her lazily, that slow smile curving his lips and promising another bone-melting kiss later.

Laney felt like she was walking on clouds as she rode next to him in his big SUV, as he ordered the exact kind of pizza she liked from Just a Pie, as he asked her about her resolutions for the new year.

"Oh, I don't know," she said. "Just trying to survive." She hadn't told him anything more about her money troubles, and she wouldn't unless they got really serious. Like, diamond ring serious. "Make sure Bailey's happy. That kind of thing."

"She said she wanted a new puppy."

Laney scoffed. "Yeah, that's not going to happen. I'll have to get up in the middle of the night with it, and I'm too old for that."

Graham gave her a peculiar look, his right eye squinting a bit more than his left.

"I can see you forming a question." She lifted her soda to her lips and waited. Graham usually didn't hesitate to vocalize what he was thinking, something Laney liked. If she was too old to get up in the middle of the night with a new puppy, she was definitely too old to play games.

"Would you get up in the middle of the night with a baby?"

She choked and flinched, soda spewing from her mouth and slopping onto the back of her hand.

Graham's face colored, but he gazed at her evenly. "You're the one who mentioned marriage and that you didn't want another man abandoning you and Bailey." He shrugged like this conversation was no big deal, but Laney felt like she'd just sprinted up the hill to his place.

"I, well, to be honest, I'd never thought about it."

"Having more kids?"

"Yes. In fact, I never thought I'd get married again."

Graham stuffed his hat lower onto his head and ducked his chin toward the table, hiding his eyes. Laney didn't like that, but she felt powerless to say the right thing.

"What about you?" she asked. "You're forty years old and unmarried."

"Thanks for pointing it out."

"I didn't think it bothered you."

He looked up. "It doesn't. It...didn't."

Laney felt like he'd splashed cold water in her face. "What are we talking about?" She'd liked Graham forever. Sure, their paths had diverged for years, and while she hadn't obsessed over him, the moment he'd moved back to Coral Canyon, her heart had been singing for him.

"We're just talking."

"Do you want children?"

He looked thoughtful for a moment, and then he nodded, that adorable ruddiness coming back into his face. "I think I do."

And Bailey probably wouldn't be enough for him. Laney bit the inside of her cheek, wondering if she could have another baby. If that was even possible at her age. If she should even risk it. She knew about the issues and birth defects that came later in life when women got pregnant.

"Noted," she said coolly, hoping she didn't come off as too icy. But kids? With Graham Whittaker? She hadn't even spent a second thinking about it, and she needed more time to process.

They ate, and he drove her to the ranch, where she was just going to run the bag in, dump everything in the laundry basket, and come right back out.

But a strange truck sat in her snowpacked driveway. "Who is that?" she wondered aloud. The plates on the vehicle were from Idaho, and Laney didn't know anyone in that state.

Graham reached to unbuckle his seatbelt. "Want me to come in with you?"

Laney peered at the truck. There didn't appear to be anyone sitting in the cab. No footprints leading up the front door, but a set that went to the garage. Her pulse reacted as though she'd been hit by lightning.

"They're in my house."

Graham pulled out his phone. "I'm calling the police." He lifted the device to his ear. "You're sure you don't know who they are?"

"Could be Gentry, I suppose," Laney mused, but the thought felt false. Her sister would not return to Echo Ridge Ranch, a place she'd despised since the day she was born. "But I don't think so."

Something seethed beneath her skin, and she put her hand on Graham's arm. "Ask Sheriff Bentley to come out. Something's not right."

Who would know how to get in her house, through the garage, with the code?

Someone who's been here before, her mind whispered.

"Hi, yeah," Graham started. "I need someone to come out to Echo Ridge Ranch. There's a suspicious vehicle in the driveway Laney doesn't recognize, and it looks like a person went in her garage."

"It's Mike," she blurted out, her mind working overtime now. Desperation clawed its way up her throat, and she felt frozen in this expensive, leather seat inside Graham's SUV.

Graham looked at her, clearly trying to listen to someone on the phone and make sense of what she'd said. "Yeah, okay," he said and hung up.

"It's Mike," Laney repeated. "He'd know the garage code, and he's just arrogant enough to show up out of nowhere and go straight inside my house."

Graham frowned, his expression turning darker by the moment. He finally turned and looked at the truck in front of them again. "When's the last time you saw him?"

"Over three years ago."

"Last time you talked to him?"

"The day he left. No, the day he was served with divorce papers, a few weeks after that. He called, surprised." She gave a bitter laugh, and it hurt her throat, her chest, her stomach. She felt seconds away from seeing her lunch for a second time that day. "I told him to sign the papers or come home. He signed while we were on the phone."

Graham reached over and threaded his fingers through hers. A simple hand-hold. He squeezed, another simple gesture. "It's okay, Laney."

She looked at him, and while she wanted to believe him, she wasn't sure how she could. "I don't want him to see Bailey." Her words felt tiny, barely made of air and letters, but she said them again, louder the second time.

"He'll destroy her, and he's already done it once."

"Let's go see what he wants. Maybe he'll leave without a fuss."

Laney scoffed but reached for her seat belt anyway. "You don't know Mike McAllister."

"No, I don't, but he doesn't know me either." The beast had added a growl to the words, and a tidal wave of relief and hope hit Laney that maybe, just maybe, she could face Mike and come out the victor—as long as she had Graham at her side.

They got out of the SUV and walked through the snow to the garage. She keyed in the code and waited for the door to lift. It seemed to take an enormously long time.

She finally ducked under and took three steps before the door to the house opened, and her ex-husband stood there, a can of soda in his hand.

"There you are," he said as if she'd just run out for groceries. His eyes flicked to Graham and stuck. The two men stared at each other, and Laney had no idea what to do.

"What are you doing here?" she asked.

"Passing through." Mike never gave a straight answer, and Laney wondered if he needed money. She had no idea what he'd been up to for the last three years, and she honestly didn't care.

"Keep driving, then," she said. "We don't want to see you." She couldn't believe she'd once found him attractive. He'd put on at least twenty pounds since she'd seen him last, and his brown hair had started to lighten into gray. His blue, blue eyes glared at her, but she didn't flinch. Or breathe.

He indicated the house behind him like he owned the place. "I like what you've done with the place."

"The Sheriff is on his way," Graham said. "You should probably leave."

Mike looked like he might snarl. Then his face smoothed over and he leaned against the doorway and took a long drag of his soda. "Karl Bentley is coming? I think I'll stay and say hello to an old friend." With that, he turned and went back into the house, letting the door slam closed behind him.

Laney couldn't move. Her legs felt numb, and she wanted to turn around and go back to the lodge. Anywhere Mike wasn't. What was he *doing* here?

And more importantly, how could she get rid of him before he destroyed everything she had—again?

CHAPTER 16

G raham couldn't seem to let go of Laney's hand. She
turned toward him. "It's all right." She tipped up
onto her toes as if she'd kiss him right there. He caught the
sweet scent of her skin as she pressed her cheek to his.

"Will you please make sure Bailey is okay? I'll be back
as soon as I can." She settled back on her feet, her grip on
his fingers tight, tight.

He ducked his head and angled his hat toward the door
just in case Mike reappeared. "How will you get back?"

"I'll call you."

"No." He shook his head, not caring if he was going to
be labeled a beast. "I'll wait in the car. Heck, I'll come in
with you." The desperation he'd held back swelled, rose,
and threatened to choke him.

"I can handle Mike McAllister."

"I know you can." He glanced toward the door, but it

remained stubbornly shut. "You just shouldn't have to. Not by yourself."

Lord, he prayed as he watched the indecision march across her face. *Please let me help her.* How, he didn't know. But he knew God did, and that He hadn't inserted Laney into Graham's life for no reason.

"I'm coming in with you." He faced the door and even took a step toward it. "Come on. Let's get this over with."

She went with him, but they were both walking pretty slowly. "He probably just wants money or something."

Graham grunted. Yes, he knew a lot of people who came out of the woodwork when money was involved, but he kept his stories to himself. There'd be a time for them, but this wasn't it.

Laney climbed the few steps first and opened the door, Graham right behind her. Warmth greeted them, a good sign, but so did the scent of browning beef, definitely not a good sign. He went with Laney down the short hall that led into the kitchen, where they found Mike panfrying hamburgers.

Graham felt like he was living in some sort of alternate reality. Who was this guy? What gall did he have to enter his ex-wife's house and start eating her food?

"I brought the meat," Mike said as if he could read Graham's thoughts. "I just need somewhere to crash for the night."

"Get a hotel," Laney said coldly, and Graham looked at her. He'd thought she'd been icy with him in the past, but he realized now he had no idea how bitter she could be.

He didn't blame her; he'd just never heard her speak in such a pointed tone.

"No money." Mike threw her a quick smile and went back to slicing a tomato. He stalled and turned back toward them. "How rude of me. Are you two hungry? I can throw on more burgers."

"We just ate," Laney said. "The furnace has been out, so I was dropping off my clothes and we're headed back to the lodge."

A huge grin stretched Mike's face, but it wasn't borne of happiness. Graham stiffened and took a half-step to put himself partially in front of Laney. Something wasn't right with this guy.

"I didn't know the furnace was out."

"There's a lot you don't know," Laney said. "And you can't stay here."

"Why not? You just said you'll be at the lodge."

"Because I pay the mortgage. It's my house. And I don't want you here, not even for a night." She folded her arms and cocked her hip. "Sheriff Bentley is on his way here, and he will escort you off my property."

Mike seemed like he didn't have a care in the world. He finished smearing mayonnaise on his bun and then slid the burger straight from the pan onto it. He layered lettuce, tomato, and avocado on top and smashed the whole thing together with the top bun.

As he took his first bite, Laney said, "Mike," in a warning voice Graham had also never heard. Watching the man eat introduced a level of disgust into Graham's life he hadn't felt in a while.

The other man finished chewing and swallowed just as someone knocked on the garage door.

Graham's heart leapt, as the situation was about to get real.

"Sheriff's here," Laney said in a smug voice, and she turned to go let him in. Graham didn't want to take his eyes off Mike until the man was in cuffs. Or headed down the road, his tail tucked between his legs. Graham wasn't sure either would happen, and his anxiety sprang around inside him.

"Laney," Mike said, and Graham never wanted to hear the man speak again. "One night. You give me this one night, and you'll never see me again."

She turned back to him, her expression wary. Graham felt the same unease dripping through him.

"But if you let that Sheriff in and make me leave, I promise I'll make your life difficult."

Graham believed him. He wasn't sure what kind of man Laney had married seven years ago, but the man in front of them wasn't to be trifled with.

"Difficult?" Laney marched back toward him. "Mike, my life has been difficult for years. No one to help with Bailey. A ranch on the brink of financial collapse." She took two menacing steps toward him with every sentence.

In that moment, Graham wasn't sure who he was more afraid of. Her or Mike.

She held up a third finger. "A furnace that's about to go out. Winter ranching by myself. *Everything* by myself. You send no money, no cards, no gifts. How much more difficult can my life get?" She stood chest-to-chest with him, a fact that made Graham very, very nervous.

"One. Night," Mike hissed. "Get the Sheriff to go away. Go back to your lodge. I'll be gone in the morning."

Several seconds of silence followed.

She finally asked, "Are you in trouble with the law?"

The man's blue eyes blazed with angry fire, and Graham stepped forward, tugging Laney backward and putting himself between the two of them. "Laney," he said, but she wouldn't look at him. "It's one night. Let him stay. You two will be safe at the lodge."

He wasn't sure why he felt like he needed to get her away from Mike, or let the man stay in the house, but Graham knew it like he knew the sun would rise tomorrow.

"Laney."

She finally tore her gaze from Mike and looked at Graham. He squeezed her shoulders. "Let him stay." He didn't mean to beg, but that was how his voice sounded.

"Listen to your boyfriend," Mike said, the squelching sound behind him indicating that he'd taken another bite of his burger.

"Don't tell me what to do." Laney stepped away from Graham, anger evident in every move. "Neither of you. No one tells me what to do." Her chest heaved and she looked back and forth between Graham and Mike.

Graham held up his hands in surrender and decided to pray again. He wasn't even sure what words to use, but trusted that the Lord would be able to hear his pleadings anyway.

Mike laughed. "Good thing you brought him in with you." He shook his head. "She's tougher than you are, man."

Graham faced Mike and said, "There are different kinds of strength."

"Sure, whatever."

The Sheriff knocked again and called, "Laney?"

"Get rid of him," Mike said, returning his attention to his food.

As much as Graham didn't want to, he agreed with Mike. They needed to get rid of Karl if they wanted to get rid of Mike. Laney looked at him, and Graham gave a slight nod.

She marched down the hall and pulled open the door a fraction of an inch. "Hey, Sheriff," she said, her voice honey-sweet. "Sorry for the call. It's my sister. She just had a rental and I didn't recognize the truck."

Low murmurs came from the Sheriff, and Laney said, "Yes, I'm sure. Sorry to make you come all the way out here." A moment later, the door closed and Laney returned to the kitchen.

Mike stood there, eating, like he didn't have a care in the world. But Graham knew he did. He was in trouble, somehow, and Graham had plenty of resources to find out what kind. He pressed his lips together and watched the other man, wishing the answers would just materialize on his forehead.

"You'll be gone by breakfast," Laney said. "And that comes early on a ranch."

"Gone by breakfast," he said in a bored voice and turned to put his plate in the sink.

"Come on, Graham," Laney said. "Let's get my bag and get out of here."

Graham followed her outside and stood guard at the bedroom door while she ducked inside to do whatever she needed to do. Mike didn't try to interact with either one of them, and as they drove back up the hill to the lodge, Laney said, "I sort of wish the furnace wasn't working again."

Graham started to chuckle, but Laney began crying, and that made his whole heart shrivel. "Hey," he said, pulling over. "Hey, hey, sh. It's okay." He gathered her as close as he could with the console between them, and stroked her hair. "It's okay."

Maybe if he said it enough times, it would come true.

———

"I DON'T KNOW," HE SAID FOR THE TENTH TIME. USUALLY Graham liked Beau and his relentless questions. Usually they were directed at someone besides him. Eli, Stockton, and Andrew had taken over the theater room for the evening, and a long six-foot table held more snacks than even he and his brothers could eat.

Graham bent over and lined up his pool cue with the ball. He and Beau had left the movie fifteen minutes ago, and it had only taken his brother thirty seconds to get Graham to spill the beans about Mike McAllister down the hill at Echo Ridge Ranch.

"You should go with her again tomorrow," Beau said.

"I will." Graham breathed out and didn't inhale again, striking the cue ball solidly and sending it toward the striped ball he needed to knock into the corner pocket. It sank nicely, and he straightened. Any other time, and he'd be satisfied with this performance. But tonight, nothing seemed to bring a smile to his face.

Laney had eaten dinner with everyone, and then complained that she didn't feel well and gone upstairs. He'd thought at least a hundred times about going up and knocking on her door, just to make sure she was okay.

Bailey was in the theater room, practically inseparable from Stockton, and while she knew she'd be going back to her house in the morning, she'd already asked Graham if she could stay for just one more day.

He hadn't told Laney, and he'd chuckled at Bailey and told her to ask her mom.

"Your turn," Graham said, and Beau shoved his phone in his pocket. He walked around the table once, and then positioned himself to hit the solid red three-ball. He scraped the table and the cue ball barely moved, lightly touching the red ball.

Graham laughed, and Beau scowled at him. "Some of us have day jobs."

"I work all the time." Graham was several strokes ahead, and he could mentally see the next three moves that would win him the game. Beau had an analytical mind, one good with numbers and figures and remember small facts no one ever needed to know.

Graham had a degree in computer science, and he

solved problems for a living. Or, at least he used to. He supposed his work for Springside Energy was about solving problems too, just in a different way. A different type of problem, as people couldn't be reprogrammed when they acted in ways he didn't like.

"I don't like him," Graham announced.

"No," Beau said. "I don't suppose you would. You do like Laney, though." He was almost asking, and Graham lined up his next shot, his thoughts tumbling over just how much he liked Laney.

He sank the striped thirteen and looked at his brother. "I really like Laney."

Beau grinned and nodded. "You've never been too serious about women before."

"What does that mean? I've had plenty of girlfriends."

"Exactly that. Girlfriends come and go like waves on the shore for you."

Graham lifted his chin. "I guess I've never really seen the point of a serious relationship."

Beau set his cue stick back in the holder, apparently forfeiting the game. "And now? I mean, you seem serious with Laney."

"I am."

"So you're in love with her."

"No." Graham leaned over and put the next ball in the end pocket. "I don't think I've ever been in love, but I think I'd know what it felt like." He looked at his youngest brother. "Wouldn't I?"

"I have no idea. I'm married to my job, remember?" He drifted over to the snack table and picked up a barbecue beef bundle. After he bit into it, he moaned and said, "Celia is the best."

Graham smiled, shook his head, and sank the last ball. A raging monster lived in his chest, and it only took him until he racked his own cue stick to label it as jealousy. He didn't want Mike anywhere near Laney or Bailey, and New Year's morning couldn't come fast enough.

CHAPTER 17

L aney found four arrest warrants for a Mike McAllister. Whether it was the right one or not, she wasn't sure. An article out of Dallas said a Mike McAllister had lost his driver's license after three arrests for driving under the influence.

"Can't be him." Laney looked up from her laptop, the darkness beyond the window a huge deterrent in her insane idea to sneak out and spy on Mike. What was he doing in her house? What condition would she find it in when she showed up in the morning? Would he really be gone?

Everything inside her body felt coiled tight, and she pushed her breath out in an attempt to relax. Problem was, she wasn't sure she even knew how to take things as they came. She liked schedules and lists and routines, and having Mike show up out of nowhere was definitely not something she knew how to deal with.

Neither was having a real relationship with Graham, if she were being honest with herself. But that was a mine-field she wanted to navigate.

She returned her attention to her computer, but another thirty minutes of Internet searching came up with nothing nefarious for Mike, as far as she could tell. Maybe if he didn't have such a common name, she'd be able to find something concrete. Some sort of evidence.

"What would you do with it?" she asked herself. She'd sent the Sheriff away, providing Mike with sixteen hours of unsupervised access to her house. "What if he does some-thing illegal at the ranch?"

Didn't matter. Laney shook the thoughts away. He'd be gone by morning, and she and Bailey would be back in their homestead, and she could get back to normal life.

She paced over to the door and paused with her hand on the knob. She should go downstairs and get involved in the New Year's Eve party. Bailey was down there, and she couldn't rely on Meg to watch her daughter all the time. Plus, Graham was probably—

She yelped as someone knocked on the door. She snatched at the knob and yanked the door open to find the man she'd just been thinking about standing in the hall.

"Hey." He gathered her into his arms, either not real-izing how quickly she'd opened the door or not caring. "How are you? Feeling better at all?"

"Yes, much better."

"Celia told me I should bring up some tea, but honestly, I think I'd probably drop it and shatter everything." He smiled, the gesture warm and flowing over her. "So I came up to see if you'd come down to the kitchen for tea."

"Do you actually drink tea?" She kept her arms wrapped around his strong back, enjoying the nearness of him, the comfort his presence brought. She'd enjoyed being married, and Mike hadn't always been completely self-centered and involved in things beyond his intellectual capabilities.

Graham laughed, and Laney basked in the sound of it. "No, I don't drink tea. But I do drink hot chocolate or coffee, and if there's tea, there's probably some of those."

"Probaby both, if I know Celia."

Graham tucked her into his side and said, "Come downstairs. I'm worried about you."

"I'm okay." She'd broken down in front of him, something Laney hadn't done in years. Sure, she cried from time to time, always behind closed doors, always when Bailey was sound asleep or sufficiently occupied in the house while Laney worked in the barns.

But she'd just lost it in front of Graham. Clung to him while she wept, let him hold her while he whispered kind things to her, and left all kinds of wet stains on his coat by the time she pulled herself together.

She'd kept her eyes averted for a while after that, but her humiliation didn't last long. People cried, and she couldn't be expected to have nerves of steel.

The mood in the kitchen bubbled, along with the two steaming pots of water. Celia jumped up from the bar, where she was studying a notebook with a pencil behind her ear. She swept the reading glasses off her face and embraced Laney. "There you are. Come, have some tea."

"I'm thinking hot chocolate," Laney said, squeezing Celia's bony shoulders to let her know she appreciated the concern. "Is that possible?"

"I think you've been here long enough to know what's possible." Celia gave her a motherly smile and busied herself with the hot chocolate. Laney got out the mugs and spoons, along with a bag of mini marshmallows. When she set the treat on the counter, she caught Graham watching her.

"What?" she asked.

"I'm just glad you're here." He lifted one powerful shoulder in a shrug. "You fit."

Laney opened her mouth to respond, but she couldn't vocalize anything. She'd wanted to fit with Graham for so long. Even as kids, she'd known he was on a different level than her. He'd been so full of life, same as he was now.

So quick to make big plans for himself. So easy to tease, and so easy to laugh with, and so easy to fall in love with.

Laney sucked in a breath when she thought the word *love*. She ducked her head and focused on spooning chocolate powder into the hot water Celia ladled up for her. She could see the ten-year-old Graham in her mind. The eighteen-year-old she'd had a crush on. And the man he'd become now.

She liked all of them, and it was possible that she could very easily fall in love with him. She took a sip of her hot chocolate and added another few marshmallows. Maybe she was already in love with him.

———

SHE WOKE BEFORE DAWN, SURPRISED SHE'D BEEN ABLE TO FALL asleep at all. After the hot chocolate tasting in the kitchen, she'd gone downstairs with Graham and let herself eat appetizers and one-bites, laugh with the Whittaker brothers, and stroke Bailey's hair after the girl fell asleep only twenty minutes before midnight.

When the clock had struck twelve, she'd gotten her New Year's kiss with Graham, amidst a chorus of catcalls from his brothers. She hadn't minded, but Graham had only kissed her for a few moments before he'd laughed and thrown a handful of marshmallows at his jeering brothers.

He'd given her a proper *welcome-to-the-New-Year* kiss outside her bedroom after walking her up the steps and promising her he'd go with her to the ranch the following morning.

Laney got up and dressed, thinking she'd make the mile-long walk to Echo Ridge as the day lightened. Get some chores done in the barn, feed the chickens, and then approach the house after she was sure the truck was gone.

"You're not going alone."

She sucked in a breath and pressed one palm over her heart as a figure rose from the couch in the foyer. Impossibly tall and wide, it couldn't be anyone but Graham.

"I knew you'd try to sneak out and go by yourself."

"No," Laney said automatically. "I hadn't planned that specifically. I just couldn't sleep."

He shrugged into his jacket and jangled a set of keys at her. "I'll drive."

"I'm going to do ranch chores first."

"Great. Maybe I'll pick up some pointers." He slung his arm around her shoulders and guided her away from the front door and toward the garage. It was no good to argue with him; Graham did what he wanted, and the thought struck fear right behind Laney's rapidly beating heart.

Graham did what he wanted.

And what happened when he didn't want her anymore?

Laney pushed the thought out of her mind and replaced it with *He's not Mike. He's not Mike*, for the duration of the short trip down to the ranch.

The offending truck was still in the driveway, and the house appeared to be asleep. "Oh, my goodness," she said, another thought hitting her with the force of gravity. "Where do you think he slept?" The homestead had four bedrooms, and she could only hope he'd taken a bed in one of the spare rooms. The thought of having him in her personal space sent a shiver down her spine.

"No matter what, it'll be okay," Graham said.

"Go around to the barn." She pointed past the driveway, and Graham continued around the property to the barns in the back. They worked together, side-by-side, and Laney let herself daydream at what life with him could be like.

He could lift twice as much as her, making the feeding go doubly fast. He stroked the horses as he went past, the same way she did. She caught him muttering a few things to Starlight, but when she asked the horse, she didn't get any of the secrets.

"Barely seven-thirty," he declared when they got the work finished. "Should we try the house?" He stood in the doorway of the main barn and faced the back of the homestead.

"Yes." She squared her shoulders and took a deep breath. "It's my house."

"Laney." Graham stepped in front of her. The look in his eyes made her pause. So intense. So serious. "I think he's dangerous, Laney. I don't think we should go in there if he's still there."

"I can handle—"

"No," Graham said. "There are some fights you fight with fists, and some with brains. This is one we use our brains for." He cast a quick glance back to the house, but it was still impossible to tell if anyone moved about inside.

"I'm not trying to tell you what to do." He faced her again. "But it's a feeling I've had since I laid eyes on your ex-husband. He's…unstable. And while I know you can handle him, you shouldn't have to."

Laney didn't know how to feel. He said the most beautiful things, and they all made sense to her. She knew her judgment was clouded when it came to Mike, so he said, "All right. Let's circle back around the front."

They did, and the truck was gone. Laney barely waited for Graham to come to a stop before she leapt from his SUV. The time it took for the garage door to lift seemed like an eternity, but she finally stepped into the house.

"I expected it to feel different," she said, moving into

the kitchen. "He left his mess." She wanted to pick up the plate he'd eaten off of last night and throw it on the floor. She opened the fridge, not sure what she expected to find, but all her bottles of salad dressing and that old container of cottage cheese wasn't it.

Graham stayed by her side as she moved through the other rooms in the house, so he was right next to her when she discovered where Mike had slept—a guest bedroom in the basement. Thankfully.

"It really does seem as though he simply slept here," she said, trying to get a noseful of some scent she couldn't smell. So he hadn't smoked in the house. Or seemingly anything else nefarious.

Graham let her go through her bedroom alone, and when she came out, he said, "I have my people on it."

"On what?"

"Finding out what's going on with Mike."

"I looked online last night."

"My people can…do more than Internet searches."

Of course they could. "Must be nice." She didn't mean to sound so snappy, but Graham just gazed at her evenly.

"It is."

Laney felt the fight go out of her, and she wanted to sag to the floor and cry again. Thankfully, Graham seemed to sense this need in her, and he wrapped his arms around her and held her up.

"Let's get cleaned up in the kitchen, and then I'll bring you and Bailey down, let you get settled." He held her at arm's length and studied her from under the brim of that cowboy hat. "Okay?"

Laney looked into the depths of his eyes, beyond relieved that Graham was here, helping her, holding her. She nodded. "Okay."

He swept his lips across her forehead, a quick touch that made her feel...loved. "Okay."

CHAPTER 18

Graham got Laney settled. He got his brothers back on airplanes headed back to their homes, with promises from them to be back in Coral Canyon as soon as they could. Eli had projects to wrap up, and a house to sell, and arrangements to work out with his nanny. Andrew likewise had obligations he had to figure out before he could come back, and Graham didn't like how empty and silent the lodge was once everyone had gone.

With January came regular life, with working out in the morning, feeding horses before breakfast, and pulling sixteen-hour work days for Springside Energy.

And now he had Laney to consider as more than someone he could text when he didn't know what to do with one of his horses. She was insanely busy after being away from the homestead for so long, and their conversations took place through texts.

Graham hated talking on the phone, something he had

to do for work and couldn't seem to bring himself to do with Laney, even though he missed the sound of her voice. Sunday morning came, and he hadn't been able to see her yesterday though they'd made plans. Bailey had come down with a stomach bug, and Laney had cancelled last-minute.

So Graham got dressed in his black slacks, white shirt, and bright blue tie, positioned his cowboy hat on his head just-so, and drove himself down the hill to Echo Ridge Ranch. His brothers had shoveled the driveway and side-walk up to her front porch, and she'd kept it clean and salted though they'd had one light skiff of snow.

He knocked on the door, hoping he wasn't being too forward. Then wondering why he cared if he was. He hadn't seen her in six days, and he really didn't like living in that lodge all alone. Even having Celia, Annie, and Bree come and go wasn't enough to make the place feel like it had a soul, the way it had over Christmas.

Bailey said, "It's Graham, Momma," and a moment later, she pulled open the door. She wore a pale blue dress that made her eyes look like the inner part of a flame— bright blue. "Hey, Graham. Momma's just putting in her earrings. She said you can come in."

"Why, thank you, Miss Bailey." He grinned at her and stepped into the house, pulling the door closed behind him. The place smelled like cinnamon and sugar, and his mouth watered. "Did your momma make something for breakfast?"

Bailey giggled and slipped her six-year-old hand into his. "No, silly. I made cinnamon rolls, just like Celia taught me. Come see." She tugged him down the hall and into the kitchen, and his whole heart filed his chest, so full he thought he'd burst.

The kitchen looked like a sugar, cinnamon, and dough bomb had gone off, and Graham stopped and stared at it in mild horror. "Where was your mom while you made cinnamon rolls?"

"Feedin' the horses." Bailey sounded real proud of herself. "You want one?"

He couldn't even see something edible, but he said, "Sure," anyway. She bypassed the island, which was smeared with flour and melted butter, and used a spatula to scrape a mostly cooked roll off the sheet tray. She plopped it onto a paper plate and presented it to him with a broad smile.

It was definitely undercooked, but Graham took a big bite anyway. At least it tasted right, even if it needed a few more minutes in the oven. Or ten. He chewed and swallowed. Okay, twenty more minutes in the oven.

"Tastes great," he said, because at least that was true. Laney walked out a moment later, her heels making clicks against the hard wood and saving him from having to take another bite of the nearly raw roll.

"Hey, stranger." She slid her fingers along his jacketed forearm and a shiver moved through him. He discreetly set his plate down on the counter and grinned at her.

"Did you brush your teeth?" Laney asked Bailey.

The girl frowned, a glob of the inner part of a cinnamon roll on her finger. She licked it off and said, "Not yet."

"Well, go get it done. We don't want to be late for

church." She watched the girl skip down the hall and into the bathroom before turning back to him. "Better kiss me quick."

Graham wanted to take his time, but he didn't waste a second taking her into his arms and matching his mouth to hers. "I missed you," he murmured and kissed her again. "I was hoping we could go to church together." Another kiss.

"You aren't worried about the town gossip?"

He kissed her again, his need for her almost insatiable. Something banged down the hall, and Laney stepped away from him, smoothing down her blouse, then her skirt, and finally her hair.

"You cut your hair," he said, reaching for the ends of it.

"Just a little," she said.

"At least six inches."

"It was getting too long." She smiled at him, and he found a pretty blush in her face. "And wow, you're a brave soul to eat that cinnamon roll."

"It just needed more time in the oven."

"Teeth brushed," Bailey announced, and Graham spun around, hoping she hadn't heard him.

"Great," Laney said. "Graham's driving us to church."

Once they were loaded up, Graham wished he owned a truck so he could have Laney's leg pressed right against his. Her perfume and her presence filled the SUV, but he wanted to hold her hand, feel the warmth of her body, and kiss her at every stop sign.

As it was, he made small talk about his brothers, asked about her mother, and engaged Bailey in a conversation about a school project she was doing about Martin Luther King for the upcoming holiday.

The church sat on the corner of Ponderosa and Third, a quaint, old building made of pink brick. Additions had been put on the back and north side for additional classrooms, and a large, field stretched toward a copse of trees. The pastor's wife held potlucks in the summer on that field, and relay races, and barbecues.

Graham liked being part of this community, and as he walked into the church, his hand securely in Laney's, more than a few people looked his way. He didn't mind. He was used to staring whenever he left the lodge, as it didn't happen often.

Usually at church, though, people had gotten used to him being there. No, he didn't say much, but neither did a whole lot of other cowboys in Coral Canyon.

"You survived the storm," a woman said, and Graham turned toward the sound to find Bonnie standing there beaming at him. "Come sit by us. Hello, Laney." She positively beamed at the pair of them, and Graham almost rolled his eyes.

Bonnie bounced her baby boy on her hip and gestured. "Come on, come on. Sam will be glad to see you."

Graham looked at Laney, who shrugged slightly. So he followed Bonnie into the chapel and down to almost the front. "Really?" he hissed to his friends. "Could we be any more on display?"

"Scoot over, Sam," Bonnie said in a voice she couldn't think was quiet. "Graham and Laney are here with Bailey."

Surprise streamed across Sam's face, but he collected the diaper bag and moved down the bench a bit. Not nearly enough, but another family had already taken up the other half. Graham squeezed himself onto the bench, as did Laney and Bailey.

Well, he'd gotten his wish of Laney's leg flush against his, her hand gripping his, but he wasn't going to kiss her. Not here on the third row where every busybody in town could see. Not in church at all—unless they'd just said "I do," and she was now his wife.

Wife.

The word bounced around inside his head, making it hard to hear the pastor's sermon. Finally, Graham pulled himself together and managed to hear the last ten minutes of Pastor Landy's message. The pastor was younger than him, something Graham appreciated, as he felt like the man understood what it was like to live in today's world.

Though Graham hadn't heard the whole thing, he'd gotten the gist of the message—the Savior loved and accepted everyone, even the sinner. They had the same responsibility.

Graham thought about Mike. It was hard to love and accept him. And forgiving him? Graham had only met the man once, and he hadn't liked what he'd done to Laney.

You're still a work-in-progress, he told himself. The meeting ended, and he spoke with Sam and Bonnie for a few minutes.

"You three should come to dinner," Bonnie said, an abnormally huge smile on her face.

"Oh, we—"

"Yeah, that would be fun," Laney interrupted him. She stood and ushered Bailey into the aisle. "We'll wait for you in the lobby." With that, she left, and Graham watched her go until she was out of earshot. Then he turned back to Bonnie.

"I'm forty years old," he growled. "You're embarrassing me."

Bonnie trilled out a laugh and patted Graham's arm like he was her son. "You're doing just fine. She held your hand for the whole meeting."

"Stop it," he said, though a sliver of happiness threaded through him. "She seems to like me, right?"

Bonnie sobered, though the sparkle in her eyes didn't go out. "Graham. Of course she likes you. I told you the two of you would be good together."

"I know." Her suggestion had plagued him for weeks, but he wasn't going to tell her that. "Okay, well, now that we're back to normal life, I don't get to see her much. So I'll see you guys later."

"Graham?" Sam stood, the diaper bag over his shoulder making him into such a dad. "Just be yourself."

Graham nodded and made his way toward the lobby, which seemed to swarm with people. Laney stood near her mother, talking, and Graham joined them.

"Afternoon, ma'am." He tipped his hat at her mother. "Would you like to join us for lunch today?"

"What's Celia making?"

"Oh, she's off today." He leaned down, a smile on his face and pure joy in his heart. "But she left a pizza noodle casserole in the fridge."

"I love that stuff," Bailey said, and Graham chuckled.

"Me too, kid," he said. "Me too."

———

DAYS LATER, MOTHER NATURE DECIDED WYOMING DIDN'T have enough snow. Somehow, six feet didn't satisfy her, and Graham trekked through the falling flakes to the barn to make sure his animals had enough to eat and drink and would stay cozy in the stables. He thought of Laney, and as soon as he made it out of the weather, he texted her to offer his help.

I'd love that, she responded. *I'll wait for you to come down.*

So while he had reports to read and three phone calls from the general manager of Springside to return, he methodically went through what it took to maintain his animals and then he drove down to Laney's house.

He knocked at the same time he opened the door, calling, "Laney? Bailey?"

"In the kitchen," Laney called.

Graham closed the door, hoping he hadn't let in too much cold. Something didn't feel quite right in the house, but he found Laney spreading caramel popcorn on a long sheet of waxed paper on the island.

"Mm, this looks good." But he didn't snatch a chunk of the warm treat. He wrapped his arms around Laney and buried his face in the hollow of her neck while she giggled. He couldn't believe how right it felt to be with her, how easy it was.

None of his other relationships had been this simple,

this carefree, this wonderful, and he wondered if it was *too* easy.

"Stop it," she said. "Bailey's right over there."

But the little girl lay asleep on the couch. Graham kissed Laney and said, "Well, get dressed so we can go get your horses fed. It's really coming down out there."

She did, and they got her farm all taken care of. He liked working with her, liked watching her whisper to the horses and talk to the barn dogs like they were real friends. He enjoyed her strength and drive, and as they walked back to the house, he thought he might be in love with Laney McAllister.

She opened the back door and entered the house, along with a gust of wind. Graham followed her, glad for the warmth inside.

But it wasn't right. It wasn't warm enough.

Laney seemed to notice too, because she said, "I need to check the furnace." She kept her coat and boots on as she went downstairs, and a few minutes later, she came back up wearing a worried look.

"It's out," she said. "The pilot light is out and I can't get it back on." She picked up her phone and started dialing.

"So you'll just come up to the lodge," he said.

She shook her head, pressed her lips together, and said, "Hey, Mom. Can Bailey and I come stay with you tonight? My furnace is out."

CHAPTER 19

Laney would not cry in front of Graham again. Oh, no, she would not. Her mom said something—Laney's basic functions of breathing seemed to be working, but nothing else. Just like her stupid furnace—and she said, "Yeah, okay."

All she could think about was how much a new furnace would cost. And it was only mid-January and her hay supply would have to be supplemented with purchased feed, as she wouldn't be able to make it stretch to the summer.

No matter how much she worked, she couldn't get enough hay in, didn't have enough money, couldn't find the strength she normally reached down deep and grasped.

A sob stuck in her chest, and she took a few steps away from Graham and Bailey, sitting on the couch. She said something into the phone as if she was still on the call, and then she ducked into her bedroom.

She barely had the wherewithal to close the door before she dropped to her knees and let the phone fall to the floor. Surprisingly, her tears didn't come. Just pure desperation mixed with quite a large dose of panic.

Tipping her face toward the ceiling, she asked, "What should I do?"

Life had never quite beaten her so badly. She didn't want to take Bailey and go into town, because it was a twenty-minute drive out to the ranch. And that was an hour each way, something she had to do twice every day. She didn't have time for that.

But she wouldn't move back into the lodge with Graham, especially since there was no one else there anymore. Their relationship seemed too intimate for that, and it simply didn't feel right.

The cabin came into her mind. It had heat, a huge fireplace, a small kitchen, and was located much more conveniently.

With this new idea lifting her spirits, she thanked the Lord for His help and got to her feet. Several seconds passed before she felt like she could face this new challenge, before she could return to the living room and set things in motion.

Graham would help her pack a cooler and whatever she needed from her pantry. If she asked him, he'd probably go to the grocery store for her. Or at least send Celia. That amended thought brought a tiny smile to her face, but when she stepped into the living room, Bailey sat on the couch alone.

"Where's Graham?" Laney asked.

Bailey didn't even look up from her tablet. "I don't know."

Annoyance flowed through Laney now, and that horrible anxiety that was never far from the surface these days. For months now, if Laney were being honest. Hadn't she been praying for a miracle for months?

"Did he leave?"

"His phone rang."

Laney strode toward Bailey, ready to rip that tablet from her hands. "Can you put that thing down?"

Bailey lowered the tablet at the sharp tone in Laney's voice. She pressed her eyes closed for a moment and tried to calm down, tried to think.

"Okay," she said with a long sigh. "We can't stay here. The furnace is out. We're going to the cabin, so go pack a bag."

Bailey blinked at her, her childlike innocence endearing. "How long will we be there?"

"I don't know, honestly." Laney was toying with the idea of staying indefinitely. She couldn't afford a new furnace until the fall at the earliest, and they didn't need this huge homestead to be happy.

She looked out the back windows, expecting to see Graham on the deck, but he wasn't there. "Go on." She could do this herself. She'd done plenty of hard things over the years. "I'm going to pack up some food."

Her heart wailed that Graham had abandoned her right when she needed him most. *That's not true*, she told herself as she loaded milk, eggs, and butter into a cooler. But he didn't return, and when she opened the garage to put the cooler in the back of her truck, his SUV didn't sit in the driveway.

She pulled out her phone and sent him a text. *Where did you go?*

She'd never known Graham to have his phone more than six inches from him, but he didn't answer immediately. Laney went back in the house and packed a bag with enough to keep her going for over a week. The cabin didn't have a washer or dryer, but she could go to the Laundromat.

She hauled out dog food, toiletries, two boxes of food, and her and Bailey's bags. By the time she was ready to go, the house was definitely chilly, darkness was falling, and Graham still hadn't answered.

Laney pressed against the tears and reached her hand toward Bailey. "Come on, bug. Call the dogs and let's go."

Graham answered hours later with only a few words: *Work emergency. Call you later.*

Laney had to accept it, the same way she'd accepted Mike's decision to leave her and their toddler on a ranch much too big for them to take care of by themselves. But she'd done it for years now, and she would keep doing the best she could.

She knew Graham worked a lot. He was the CEO of a very large energy company that had faced its share of controversy over the years. She couldn't expect him to spend Thursday evenings doing her chores—or any evening really.

But by the time she'd finally loaded everything she'd packed into the cabin, she was exhausted mentally, physically, and spiritually. She helped Bailey get ready for bed, and then she crawled into a hot bath, utterly spent.

And finally, the tears came and she let them fall into the bathwater, where at least they were hidden.

————

GRAHAM DID NOT CALL HER LATER THAT NIGHT, NOR THE next day, nor over the weekend. Laney had sent him a few texts that also went unanswered, and she felt like someone had reached into her chest and ripped out her heart.

Half of her still believed he'd show up on Sunday morning, wearing those delicious church clothes with his cowboy hat, and ask her to go to church with him. He didn't, but he did finally send a message that said, *I had to leave town. Text me what Pastor Landy says?*

Leave town? she messaged back. *Where are you?*

Energy Summit in New York. I'll explain it all later.

Of course he couldn't be bothered to provide proper explanations when *she* needed them. He'd always done everything on his timetable, and bitterness accompanied Laney as she readied herself for church.

By the time the pastor started speaking, Laney wanted to leave. She was used to sitting by herself, but not used to people staring at her, unasked questions in their eyes. *Where's Graham this week? Did you two break up already?*

She hadn't kept tabs on his church attendance. She had a crush, not an obsession. But it seemed like everyone with two eyes knew he wasn't there, and especially not with her. As Pastor Landy spoke about charity and loving everyone—a repeated topic for him already in this new year—Laney managed to talk herself out of being mad and feeling abandoned.

After all, if her job required her to jet off to New York, she'd have gone. Well, maybe. Depending on how much it cost.

The bitterness had moved from her heart into her stomach, and it didn't seem fair that God had blessed others with so much money and her so little. She didn't need grandeur, pomp, or recognition. She just wanted to keep the ranch that had been in the Boyd family for four generations.

She closed her eyes as a headache started to pound in her forehead. *Please help me, Lord,* she prayed. *Help me to be grateful for what I have and find a way to get what I need.*

She didn't feel like she was being greedy for wanting a furnace that worked when it was ten below zero outside. A sense of calmness came over her, and she knew things would work out all right. She'd felt this way before—once when Graham had left Coral Canyon and they'd fallen out of touch.

And once when Mike had declared he couldn't stay in Wyoming for another day, packed a bag, and left that night.

She'd been in turmoil during both of those times and

received the comfort she needed, the strength to pick herself up and try for another day.

"That's all you need," she whispered to herself.

"What, Momma?"

"Nothing, Bay." She tucked her daughter into her side and breathed in the soft, peach scent of her hair. "Nothing."

But she just needed to get through one day at a time.

The next day, she called a furnace repairman, who confirmed that the entire unit needed to be replaced. She did her chores, and worked with Bailey on her math, and made it through the day.

Cabin life wasn't fun, and she busied herself by texting Graham, hoping whatever meeting he was in would be boring enough to get him to respond.

The sting when he didn't was too much for her to bear along with everything else, so she kept her phone in her pocket the following evening. And the next night too.

Thursday came again, a whole week since she'd seen Graham, heard his voice, or had any real conversation with him at all.

She juggled Bailey, homework, pets, animals, the ranch, making dinner, and housework as best as she could. Every day that passed was another day she'd made it through. By the weekend, Bailey had come down with something and Laney was up all night and all day with her while she ran a fever and threw up anything she ate.

Laney got up on Sunday morning, still tired and beyond frustrated. How long would the Lord let this go on? She couldn't think about Graham for another minute, and yet, he was always there, taking up space and energy in her mind.

She couldn't fix the furnace, but it lingered in her brain too, taunting her, reminding her how much of a failure she was.

Bailey seemed better, but not well enough to go to church, and that was just fine with Laney. She wasn't fit to leave the cabin anyway.

"This isn't a life," she said to her reflection. She wore a pair of yoga pants and an oversized sweatshirt, the dark circles under her eyes almost a complement to the grungy clothes. "This is a terrible way to live."

Sadness enveloped her, and the very thought of having to do another round of feeding that night made her head swim and tears prick her eyes.

"I can't do this." She twisted away from her reflection and went to find her phone. She could solve some of her problems with a few texts and phone calls, and she was tired of feeling sorry for herself, tired of being so dang tired, and unwilling to live in this depressive turmoil for one more day.

"Hey, Jake," she said when the man answered. "You still lookin' for work?" She couldn't afford to pay him, not really, but she'd figure it out. She'd go to the bank tomorrow and get whatever loan she needed to pay a hired hand and get her furnace fixed. It was just money. She could make more once calf season came and she had beef and cattle to sell.

"I can just offer one shift," she told him when he'd said "Maybe."

"You choose. Morning chores or evening. I'll do the other one."

"Morning," he said, and Laney's heart soared. If she didn't have to get up and out the door, in her boots, long underwear, and coat, she could sleep in, make Bailey a real breakfast before school, and take care of the business side of the ranch better.

"Fifteen an hour okay?" she asked, praying it was. He'd come to her last spring with that offer, but she hadn't hired him. She hadn't been this desperate last spring.

"Yes, ma'am." He chuckled and added, "I got hired on at the cabinetmaker over the summer. I've been doing great there."

"I'm sure you have, Jake." At this point, Laney didn't care that he'd spent a year in jail and was a bit slow in the head. He'd never be near Bailey or alone with her, and Laney needed him.

"Tomorrow okay to start?" she asked.

"Yes, ma'am."

"Great, I'll see you in the morning. Seven o'clock."

"I won't be late."

Laney ended the call, a huge burden lifted from her shoulders. Her first thought was *I need to tell Graham*, but her second screamed louder. *He won't answer.*

He doesn't care.

Does an Energy Summit last longer than a week?

She didn't want to think about it anymore. She didn't have the head space, the mental or physical energy, or the patience.

"I deserve to come first sometimes," she said aloud to

the quiet cabin. "I deserve to be happy." And Graham had hardly ever put her first. And while the few weeks she'd spent with him as his girlfriend had made her insanely happy, she didn't want to be put on the backburner every time something came up with his job—and he had a very big, important job he'd made clear came first.

So with her heart shrinking and then pounding around inside her chest, she tapped out one more message to him.

I think it's time we call our relationship what it is: over. Good luck with your summit.

CHAPTER 20

G raham glared at Dwight, the other man's mere presence enough to put Graham in a foul mood. He'd been back in town for approximately three hours before Dwight had shown up at the lodge.

On a Saturday night, no less.

Demanding a meeting that had taken most of the night.

Graham yawned, his anger and frustration no less just because he was exhausted. "You can't keep ignoring me when I call," Dwight said. "We have things happening at Springside—important things that require the CEO's attention."

"It was a protest, Dwight. They happen about once a month."

He shook his head, his hair shaved close to the scalp staying still. "It was more than a protest. A petition has been filed, and I needed you—I need you to know about these things so we can take action on them quickly. Did you know that if we're shut down from drilling for even one day, we lose over fifty thousand dollars?"

Graham rubbed his thumb across his forehead. "I'm aware, Dwight."

"We lost two days because you wouldn't answer your phone. I can't make executive decisions about legalities," he continued. "Your father—"

"Always answered his phone," Graham finished for the general manager of Springside Energy. "I know, Dwight."

"Why didn't you answer?"

"I was busy." He gazed at the other man, daring him to ask Graham what he'd been doing. He wouldn't tell him, and Dwight seemed to know, because his shoulders fell and he sighed.

"Are we back up now?" Graham asked, his voice perfectly even.

"Yes."

Graham felt sure that Dwight would've added a "sir" to the sentence if he'd been talking to Ronald Whittaker, Graham's father. But Dwight lifted his chin, a silent dare for Graham to make him say it.

He wouldn't. "All right." He let out a long sigh. "Thank you, Dwight."

The older man tapped the stack of folders he'd put on the desk last night. "I still need these read, signed, and statements prepared. By tonight at the latest. We can't go another business day without responding."

"Tonight," Graham said, already distracted by the farm beyond the window.

"Maybe I'll stay here until you get them done."

"No." Graham stood. He couldn't survive the day with Dwight in the lodge. He thought he'd wanted company, but Dwight was completely the wrong kind. "I'll get them done. No later than six p.m. tonight. You have my word."

Dwight looked like he highly doubted Graham could deliver on his word, but he put his arms through his suit jacket and said, "All right. My wife will be wondering where I am anyway."

Graham didn't walk the other man out, his thoughts already back on Laney. He'd left suddenly, hadn't called her, and spent too long in New York getting the permits he needed. He'd never met with so many lawyers, explained his situation so many times, and had to relive the death of his father over and over again.

He definitely did not want to repeat the last ten days ever again. Ever.

He picked up his phone and found a message from Laney. She'd stopped texting after the first day, and Graham had missed her more than he could express. But the whole family—the entire Whittaker empire—lay on Springside Energy, and Graham was needed at the Energy Summit, in court, and back in Wyoming all at the same time.

He couldn't be everything to everyone.

And apparently he couldn't be Laney's boyfriend anymore.

I think it's time we call our relationship what it is: over. Good luck with your summit.

Over.

"Over?" He jammed his thumb on the call button, hoping she'd texted recently. And that she'd answer. Laney had a stubborn streak, and she did *not* like being told what to do. And she didn't answer.

"I'm coming over," he said to her voicemail and he had his coat and gloves on before he realized how he sounded.

Beastly.

Like his word would be obeyed. That he could just barge back into her life whenever he wanted, and she'd swoon she was so happy to see him.

His phone rang and he fumbled to get it out of his pocket, finally tearing the glove off and pulling the phone out on the last ring.

"Eli," Graham mumbled, his pulse settling back to normal. But he needed to talk to Eli too, so he called his brother back.

"Hey, couldn't get to the phone fast enough," he said.

"My last day is Friday," Eli said with a laugh. "It's been amazing how things have worked out here. House sold in one day. One day, Graham!" The elation in his brother's voice wasn't hard to hear.

"That's great, Eli." And Graham meant it. He needed his brother here too. If there was more than just Graham managing things at Springside, maybe he'd have time to eat dinner—or spend time with his girlfriend.

But Eli's not coming to help with Springside, his mind whispered.

Graham pushed the thought away.

"And Meg agreed to relocate to Wyoming. I guess something about the snow charmed her."

"I can't imagine how that's possible."

"Right?" Eli laughed again. "But I'm glad. Stockton likes her."

Graham thought Eli was the one that liked Meg, but he kept that to himself. He didn't have the mental capacity to deal with women at the moment. He slowly took off his other glove and slid his coat down his arms and hung it back on the hook in the mudroom.

"So when will you be back in town?"

"We have to get packed up and get the moving company here. I'm selling a lot too, since we don't need tons of furniture." Eli continued to talk, and Graham wandered into the kitchen and sat at the bar.

He must not have participated in the conversation appropriately, because Eli finally said, "I can tell I'm boring you."

"No, not at all." If Eli ended the call, Graham wouldn't have anyone to talk to. None of his employees worked on Sundays, and Graham suddenly felt like all the space in this huge lodge was suffocating him.

"What's wrong then?"

Graham's first inclination was to keep his problems to himself. He hadn't told anyone about Erica—except Laney.

"Laney broke up with me." He wanted to hang his head and figure out how to get her back. That was something he was very good at and had done over and over in his life. Figure out what he wanted and then work until he got it.

But he had a feeling he couldn't do that when there was

another person involved. Especially someone as head-strong and intelligent as Laney.

"Oh, no," Eli said. "What happened? I thought you two were great together."

Graham scrubbed his fingers down his beard, which he'd kept short and neat while in New York. "I had to go to New York for Springside, and there were so many problems...." He let his voice trail off. He really disliked the management part of running the energy company. Maybe he should let Dwight do it now that Graham knew all the ins and outs.

He exhaled and then took a long, deep breath. "She thinks I abandoned her." It was as if a light bulb had gone off over his head. "I need to go talk to her."

"Yeah, sounds like it."

Because Graham didn't abandon anything. If he was the running type, he'd have left Coral Canyon five minutes after the funeral and left Dwight in charge of the company while he put his life back together in another tech city.

He hung up with Eli, all of his thoughts tumbling around like clothes in a dryer. "You wouldn't have survived in another tech city," he told the empty house. This place, Coral Canyon, had healed him in a way he hadn't anticipated. And moving forward with Laney was the best thing he'd done in his path back toward happiness.

"I have to get her back." With less frantic movements, he returned to the mudroom and got dressed for a long walk in the winter weather.

He went down the road, which was still covered in ice. It was a miracle he didn't fall on the mile-long walk down to Echo Ridge Ranch. Why he thought Laney would be there, he wasn't sure. His brain wasn't working properly.

Neither was her furnace, because when he let himself into the homestead, it was as cold inside as out. Well, minus the wind.

He looked at the family pictures hanging on the wall leading down to the kitchen, drinking in the happiness he found in Laney's eyes, in Bailey's smile. This was what happiness was. Family. Relationships. He had all the money in the world, but he didn't have those.

"Soon," he whispered to himself.

He pulled out his phone and called his mother. "Hey, Mom, real quick. I need the number for Steffanie Boyd."

"Steffanie? Laney's mom?"

"Yes."

A long pause came through the line, and Graham hoped she wouldn't ask why. Wouldn't ask why he couldn't just get the number from Laney.

"Let me see what I have," she finally said, and a few seconds later, she recited it to Graham. He repeated it back to her while he typed it into his note app, and then hung up before any more conversation could get going. He loved his mom, he did, but she could get talking, and Graham had a task to do.

Steffanie's line rang several times, and desperation clawed through Graham's system while he waited for her to answer or her voicemail to pick up.

She finally said, "Hello?" in a breathless voice.

"Hello, ma'am," he said, employing his polite CEO voice. "It's Graham Whittaker. I need to find Laney, and I'm wondering if she's staying with you."

"Oh, she's not, dear," Steffanie said. "She's probably at the cabin."

The cabin has power. She'd told him that just before the new year. She and Bailey probably were there, as it was close to the ranch and she could still get her work done.

"Thank you, ma'am," he said and hung up.

Thankfully the cabin was just up the hill a bit. He raised his collar and stepped back out into the wind, making his strides long so he could get to the cabin faster.

His courage took a vacation as the cabin came into view. Smoke lifted from the chimney on the roof, and two squares of light looked like yellow eyes in the twilight. He looked back toward the lodge, seriously considering just going home.

"This is for Laney," he whispered to himself. He squared his shoulders and stepped toward the front door, praying that she'd open it when he knocked.

His fist sounded like gun shots against the door, and he couldn't hear anything inside for a long time. He knocked again, determined not to leave without seeing Laney. Her truck sat in the lane, which meant she was here.

Unless she was at the ranch, working.

He knocked for a third time, finally hearing something behind the closed door. "Laney," he called. "It's Graham."

The door opened a few moments later, and she stood there wearing yoga pants and a large sweatshirt. Her hair had been knotted on top of her head, as usual. She wore no makeup, and Graham was struck speechless at her casual beauty.

"What do you want?" She spoke in that same icy tone he'd heard her use on Mike, and that simply would not do.

CHAPTER 21

Laney tried not to drink in the tall, dark, handsome sight of Graham Whittaker. She'd spent entirely too many days of her life doing exactly that.

"I did not abandon you," he said in a calm, clear voice. "I had a crazy week in—Look. It doesn't matter. I'm still as committed to this as ever." He gestured between the two of them, and Laney had to admit she liked the way the words sounded.

"This has nothing to do with you going to New York," she said.

Confusion crossed Graham's face, and his nose and cheeks were pink from the cold. She wondered how long he'd been outside, if he'd wandered around the ranch looking for her. She'd never told him she was coming to the cabin.

"Then what's it about?" he asked.

"I'm…I'm not ready for a relationship."

An edge entered his eye that spoke of suspicion. "I don't believe that."

"You can believe what you want." But her voice wavered a little, and he heard it. Graham wasn't stupid, that much was certain.

"Laney."

She loathed how he said her name with that note of condescension, as if she were being unreasonable.

"No," she said, the word exploding out of her mouth. "No. You don't get to 'Laney' me." She drew herself up tall and determined to say what she should've told Mike all those years ago. What she should've done with Graham from the beginning. Bailey would probably cry for days and stop talking to Laney, but she pushed those thoughts away. She couldn't make huge life decisions based on what her six-year-old thought about the handsome cowboy.

"I am worth your attention," she said. "I deserve to be your first priority. I know you can't give that. I know it's probably selfish and unfair of me to want it." Her emotions clogged her throat, but she pushed her voice past them anyway.

"But I do want it. And I'm tired of making excuses for you and everyone else for putting me second, or third, or last." Her chest shook; her stomach quaked. She was going to cry—again.

"I deserve explanations when I ask questions, not when you have time to give them. Bailey and I deserve someone who's going to love us, take care of us, and put us first." She shook her head and swiped angrily at her eyes. "So this has nothing to do with you physically going to New

York. This has to do with you not being able to make a phone call when you said you would."

"I'll make the phone calls," Graham said, his voice as broken as Laney felt inside.

She looked right into those dreamy eyes and wished she could erase his pain. "I don't need them now, Graham. I can take care of myself and Bailey. And while I was hoping for a partner, a friend, to lean on, I don't need it. I can do it myself."

And she could. She would.

Graham stood there, and Laney really couldn't afford to heat the wilds of Wyoming. "Goodbye, Graham." She slowly closed the door, the click of it when it latched one of the most horrifying sounds she'd ever heard.

She expected the beast in Graham to pound on the door again, call something through the wood, insist she listen to him.

Nothing happened, and when Laney finally got the nerve to peer through the window, she found him trudging down the lane, his shoulders slumped and his head bent.

She embraced her old friend misery, stumbled into the kitchen to retrieve a couple of cookies from the freezer, and collapsed onto the couch to stare at the TV without really seeing.

———

THE NEXT MORNING, JAKE WAS WAITING IN HIS TRUCK NEAR the barn when Laney arrived. He was fifteen minutes early, and Laney lifted her hand in greeting, a bit of trepidation tugging through her. She probably should've told *someone* that she'd hired the ex-con.

Her list was short, and had gotten shorter with the departure of Graham from her life. Sadness filled her. Even when she couldn't kiss Graham, she could still talk to him. Joke with him. Talk about the past with him.

Now, it felt like she'd lost a lifelong friend and her boyfriend.

"Morning, Laney," Jake said, coming toward her with an eager smile on his face. "Thank you so much for hiring me. I won't let you down." He shook her hand, his bright blue eyes reminding her so much of Bailey's.

A rush of relief spread through her, and she nodded toward the barn. "You'll mostly work in here. I have thirteen horses that need fed. Two barn cats and two barn dogs. They can run around while you work in the stables. But they have to be put back in before you go. It's too cold for them outside."

Jake nodded, his cowboy hat old and torn along one side. He asked questions and nodded as she gave directions. She worked side-by-side with him, told him about the cattle and how he'd go out and check them every other day. She used a four-wheeler for that, and the corrals weren't that far away.

"I'll check them on the other days," she said. "We watch for sickness. I'll give you something to read. Is that okay?"

"Sure, I can read."

She cocked her head at him. "Of course you can. I just wondered if you'd have time with your other job."

"I'll have my dad help me." Jake gave her a friendly smile, and Laney moved on to the chickens.

"These are Bailey's favorite animals," she said. "They hardly lay any eggs in the winter, but every once in a while you'll find one. They should be checked so they don't get nesting sores."

Laney finished the tour and the chore list, gave Jake the booklet on cattle diseases and sicknesses that were common in the winter, and headed back to the cabin. Her mother had been there to get Bailey for school, as the girl and her backpack were gone and a loaf of still-warm banana bread sat on the kitchen counter.

Laney touched it with reverence, knowing it was a symbol of her mother's insomnia that had struck particularly bad since the death of her husband. It would make great French toast tomorrow when Laney would be home with Bailey in the morning. She could make breakfast and drive her own daughter to school, and the thought made Laney smile with true joy, something she hadn't done in a while.

She cleaned out the fridge, gathered all the dirty laundry, and went into town to get errands done. She visited the Laundromat first, then the grocery store, then the bank.

When she walked through the doors, she realized she should've made the bank her first stop, because she wasn't sure she could keep her emotions in check while she begged for money.

It's not begging, she thought, glancing around. She

hadn't been inside the bank for a few years, not since she'd had the deed for the ranch redone to have her name only and all the mortgage documents had been reprocessed.

"Do you need help?" A man approached, wearing a dark suit and his hair swept to the side with quite a lot of gel.

"Yes, sir," she said. "I'm wondering about a loan."

"I can help you with that." He extended his hand for her to shake. "My name's Chris. What do you need a loan for?" He looked over his shoulder as he spoke, walking back toward a big desk that seemed entirely too impressive for a simple loan application.

"I own Echo Ridge Ranch," she said as he gestured to a chair. "And I need money for a new furnace and for payroll for my only employee."

"Small business loan," he said, taking a seat behind the ginormous desk. He bent and opened a drawer, pulling out a few sheets of paper. "We do small business loans for improvements, expenses, all of it." He pushed the papers toward her, and she could've sworn he had a manicure. She'd never seen a man with such clean, crisp hands.

She stretched across the desk and collected the papers. "Should I take these with me, and bring them back?" She could do it in the morning when she brought Bailey to school. Maybe spend an hour with her mom before the bank opened. Laney couldn't imagine such luxury, and while she still had plenty to do around the ranch, having someone take four hours of work in the morning had relieved a massive burden from her shoulders.

Maybe with Jake's help, she could get more crops

planted, put up more hay, and still be able to sleep and mother.

Hope filled her chest, and she reached for a pen. She was going to fill this application out right now and get things started. She could pick something up for dinner to save time, and enlist Bailey's help with the evening chores, and maybe she'd be able to get actual rest tonight when she slept.

Forty-five minutes later, Chris had answered all her questions, had her forms, and had promised to call her the moment her application had been processed. "Twenty-four to forty-eight hours," he said as he shook her hand again.

Laney went home and unpacked everything, folded laundry, cleaned up the kitchen, and promptly went back into town to pick up Bailey.

Every time she drove by the lodge, Laney couldn't help looking at it. Couldn't help imagining what Graham might be doing behind the decorative double doors, and what Celia might have cooked up for dinner.

This afternoon, three cars sat in the lot that hadn't been there earlier. Probably his housekeeper, his chef, and his interior decorator. A flash of jealousy made her throat tight and her foot heavier on the accelerator.

She couldn't change Graham. He'd always done what he wanted to do, and she couldn't expect him to change for her.

"Too bad you fell in love with him before you figured that out." Laney had never admitted it to herself, but it hadn't taken long for him to nestle into the soft places of her heart, what with socks on Christmas Eve, and incredible hospitality, and a family spirit she longed for in her life.

Mike hadn't ever provided a strong inclination toward family life, and Laney had changed every diaper and given Bailey every bath. But Graham wanted children, and she could imagine him as a caring, attentive father.

"When he's not working," she muttered, putting Whiskey Mountain Lodge in her rear-view mirror. She'd get over Graham. She had once before. But as she waited outside the school for Bailey to come out, she thought she might be in too deep with Graham to ever truly get over him.

She couldn't stop thinking about him and all the things he'd promised they'd do. Snowshoeing, horseback riding, swimming in the pool at the lodge. For a few days there, maybe a week, perhaps two, she'd thought her life could change. She'd thought she and Graham could have a real shot at a future together, a life of happiness, a family with a mom and a dad.

Sometimes her fantasies could get away from her.

"But not anymore," she told herself as she saw Bailey skipping toward her. She sat up straighter and put a smile on her face for her daughter. She'd keep grinning until it became genuine. Until she'd caught up and then gotten ahead on her financial obligations. Until her heart stopped hurting.

CHAPTER 22

Graham made lists for work as easily as breathing. After Laney had used her ex-husband voice on him, he'd taken a few days to wrap his head around what she'd said.

She wanted to come first. Of course, he'd been able to provide that for her during the holidays. He'd been there, lending a listening ear, giving her a shoulder to lean on, cry on, hold onto when she needed it.

He had to decide what to do with the information, and he'd been making lists of what he wanted his life to be, what he didn't want it to be, what he liked about Laney, what he could control about his job, his life, the way he treated her.

Someone knocked on his office door late in the afternoon on Friday while he reviewed one such list. Well, he hadn't exactly started the list yet. A single question sat at the top, reading *Do I love Laney?*

So it wasn't a list. Not exactly. But all of his other lists and soul-searching that week had revolved around this one question.

"Come in," he called, sliding the paper underneath a pile of folders.

Dwight came in, looking like he hadn't worked all week, or for several hours today already. "Afternoon, Graham." He could be civil, that was for sure. And he was professional through and through.

"Hey, Dwight." Graham opened the notebook where his chicken scratch stared back at him, notes about what he wanted to maintain control of and what he hoped Dwight would take on. "Thanks for coming."

The other man settled across from Graham's desk and steepled his fingers under his chin. Graham almost rolled his eyes, but he needed Dwight on his side.

"I have a few things to talk about," Graham said. "And it has to do with the running of the company."

"The running of the company?"

"I work too much," Graham said simply, unwilling to go into detail for this man he could barely tolerate. "I don't need to do everything, be everywhere. I'm hoping you'll help me put together a task list for both of us that makes my life more manageable and gives you more of the freedom you've wanted since I took over last year."

Dwight blinked at him, his hands falling to the armrests. "You're serious?"

"Of course I'm serious." Graham didn't joke about business. About much, actually. Probably another strike against him if Laney were keeping a list. Wow, he hoped she wasn't keeping a list.

Dwight leaned forward and glanced at the notebook, though Graham doubted he'd be able to read a single word of it. "All right. Let's hear what you've got."

"I'd still like to be involved in major things," Graham said. "But I want to be the big picture guy, while you're the day-to-day guy." He glanced at Dwight to see if they were still on the same page.

A light had entered Dwight's eyes, something Graham hadn't seen in a long time. "Go on."

"I want to be involved with legal. My brother's moving home to take on public relations and some marketing, and I want to work closely with him on that. But I don't want to do payroll anymore. I don't want to deal with employees, or schedules, or drill sites." Graham felt a burden lifting from him as he continued to outline what he hoped were decent plans for Springside Energy moving forward.

"I want to spend more time in the lab," he said. "Developing the robotics that could really help us make sure we're being as environmentally friendly as possible. I think that will go a long way with the public as well."

"So I'll be the general manager, and you'll be the CEO." Dwight grinned at him, and for the first time since Graham had taken over the company, he felt like he and Dwight were on the same page.

"I suppose I deserve that."

Dwight lifted one shoulder in a shrug and kept smiling. "Your father told me you were stubborn and would want to learn everything."

The breath whooshed out of him as the weight of Dwight's statement hit him. "You talked to my father about me?"

"He always knew you'd take over Springside." Dwight sobered and finally looked like a man Graham could trust with personal things and professional things.

"He died of a heart attack," Graham whispered. "When did you talk to him about this?"

"He wasn't well for a few months before his death." Dwight cleared his throat. "He didn't tell your mother. No one but me. He told me a lot of things about you and your brothers in that time."

Graham's chest pinched and he couldn't seem to get a proper breath. Dwight had known his father better than Graham had. Probably better than anyone. And Graham hadn't once thought to talk to the man about his father.

"I'm sorry," Graham said, true regret lacing through him. "You must miss my dad as much as I do."

The pain flashed across Dwight's face, and Graham couldn't believe he'd never thought of the other man as a human being with feelings before. Maybe he was just too deep into his grief, and he did like to do things his way.

His way.

Wasn't that exactly what Laney didn't like about him? Everything had to be his way. He couldn't even provide an explanation for her when she needed one.

He hadn't realized that was what he'd done, but it didn't matter. How she felt about it was what mattered. He sighed, so tired of thinking about what he'd done wrong and how he could fix it.

"I miss your father, yes," Dwight said, his voice quiet. "He was a good man and a good boss. Tough when he had to be. Kind always. Family-oriented."

Graham wanted to be just like him, and he knew if he didn't fix things with Laney fast, their time to have a bigger family than just Bailey would be lost. He compartmentalized her for the time being and continued his meeting with Dwight. After all, if he wanted to win Laney back, he had to show her that he'd made some changes in his life. Changes that would put her first—right where she deserved to be.

———

THE LAST SATURDAY IN JANUARY FOUND HIM STANDING behind his barns, looking down the hill and over the snow toward Echo Ridge Ranch. He searched the clear sky for any hint of smoke, anything to show that Laney was still at the cabin.

There was nothing, and he wondered if she'd moved back to the homestead. If she had, that meant the furnace had been fixed. He hated that he hadn't done it for her. He should've called someone from the plane as he flew to New York and replaced the whole thing.

He saw that now.

He saw a lot of things now that he'd been blind to before.

But he still didn't know how to get her back into his life. Before, when he'd needed her, he'd text her. She always came, and he wondered if she would again.

But he wasn't going to ask that of her.

He turned and went back to the lodge to get ready for his brother's arrival. Eli and Stockton and Meg were set to arrive at the airport tomorrow, and Graham wanted to have everything perfect for them when they arrived. Sure, the lodge was fun for a five-year-old who was only staying for a couple of weeks over Christmas. But it would be his nephew's home, and Graham had plans to make the boy's room exactly what it should be.

After he'd worked in the basement room, putting up a wall of Lego sheets so Stockton could create right on the walls of his room, he went outside, this time to the front of the lodge. Eli would do a full analysis on the lodge when he arrived, everything from parking to permits, but Graham felt like he should know as much as his brother. The lodge had a water feature in the front, but he'd done nothing with it in the year he'd lived there.

A truck came up the lane from the ranch, drawing his attention from the fountain, but it wasn't Laney's. A man sat behind the wheel, and he drove so slowly that Graham had several long seconds to look at his face.

Jake Langford. What in the world was he doing down at Echo Ridge Ranch?

He waved to Graham like they were old pals, and Graham lifted his hand in return. Jake was Beau's age and a little bit mentally handicapped. Graham had heard he'd been blamed for a theft a few years ago, and Beau was sure the man hadn't done it. But Jake had been confused, in the wrong place at the wrong time with the wrong people, and he'd gone to jail for thirteen months.

And now he was...doing what exactly down at Laney's?

"She's a grown woman," Graham muttered to himself. "You're not her husband, and it's none of your business."

Problem was, he wanted it to be his business. He was in love with Laney, after all.

He froze, his jaw muscle twitching. Had he just thought he was in love with Laney?

"Of course you are," he muttered, his bad mood growing though he'd come outside to get relief from the melancholy atmosphere inside the lodge. He wouldn't be this miserable if he wasn't in love with her. He wouldn't upend his entire life just to prove to her that she was the most important thing he had. Heck, she wouldn't be the most important thing he had if he didn't love her.

And with that, he decided he didn't need a big show to impress Laney. No pomp or circumstance. He just needed for her to see that he'd put her first.

Just the fact that he was wandering around the grounds, looking at defunct fountains, proved that his life had already changed. He never would've had time to do that before he'd split responsibilities with Dwight.

He gazed up into the sky, the brightness of the blue and the glinting sun making his eyes hurt to the point of watering. "Do I just go talk to her?"

The sky didn't answer. Neither did God, for that matter. But Graham felt something way down deep in his soul that whispered, *Yes, just go talk to her.*

Instead of jumping behind the wheel of his SUV, he opted to walk the mile down the road to her house. The truck sat in the garage, which was also open, and he made his way to the front door and knocked.

"Momma!" he heard Bailey shout. "It's Graham."

He winced, wishing his identity could've been a secret until Laney opened the door. But Bailey whipped it open in the next second, and she threw herself into his arms. "Graham! Did you come for my birthday?"

He hadn't even known it was the girl's birthday, but he couldn't say that. Laney appeared down the hall, an apron around her waist and the scent of freshly baked cake hanging in the air. Their eyes met, and Graham thought it would be okay to tell a lie, just this once.

"I sure did, Bay. Happy birthday."

The little girl squealed and wiggled out of his arms. He let her run ahead while he approached much slower. Bailey put on her coat and said, "Momma, I'm gonna go out with the cats for a minute, okay?"

"Okay, bug. Have fun." Laney just watched him with those green eyes, clear as glass. She looked better than he'd ever seen her, and he waited until her daughter had pulled the back door closed behind her before he spoke.

"I just saw Jake Langford leaving from down this way." Graham hooked his thumb over his shoulder, wondering why he'd started with Jake. There were so many more important things to talk about.

"I hired him," Laney said. "He does my morning chores, so I can do this kind of stuff." She walked back into the kitchen and washed her hands. "You don't have to stay for her birthday party. It's not for hours."

"I don't even have a gift for her. I can run and grab something and come back."

"That's not necessary." At least she was talking to him, and not in that ultra-cold voice.

"Laney," he said, exhaling a moment later. "I've made a few changes in my life this week, and I'd love to tell you all about them."

She barely flicked her gaze in his direction as she measured out butter, cream cheese, and powdered sugar. "Oh?"

He stuffed his hands in his pockets, no speech prepared. "I don't want to be friends."

That got her to stop and stare at him, the teaspoon of vanilla hovering above the bowl. "What?"

"I can't just be friends with you anymore." He shrugged, realizing how warm it was in the homestead. Or maybe that was just him sweating because of this conversation. "I'm in love with you, and I want to be more than friends. I want to be your partner. Your *best* friend. Your husband. Your daughter's father. Your lover. Your biggest supporter." He took a big breath. "I want to know how you got your furnace fixed, and why you had to hire Jake. I want to know everything about your ranch, and I want to help you with it."

He tried to sound less like he was reading from one of his lists, but the fact was, he had the blasted things memorized. "Because of those wants I met with my general manager this week, and I'll be working much less as he takes over more of the day-to-day tasks. I wanted you to know that. I wanted you to know I'm going to put you first. That is, if you'll take me back." He took a step forward and then settled back again.

"Please, Laney," he said. "Forgive me, and let's try again."

CHAPTER 23

Laney's heart danced around inside her chest. Graham said such lovely things, and she wanted to believe them all. Especially the part where he said he loved her and wanted to support her.

"Are you going to say anything?" he asked.

Laney blinked, her mind revolving at twice the speed now. "Yes."

Graham continued to wait, but he looked like he was about to bolt, like it was taking everything inside him to stay and listen.

"I got a loan for the furnace," she said. "We could've kept living in the cabin, but it's not really meant for long-term habitation." She filled the teaspoon with vanilla and added it to her frosting mixture.

"I hired Jake because I'm exhausted. I can't run this ranch on my own." The words were painful coming out of her mouth, but they hurt less than she'd thought they would. "I don't put in enough crops, or enough hay to last the winter. So then I'm spending money I don't have on feed and supplemental hay. If Jake's here, I can be a mom in the mornings, work around the ranch and house during the day, and Bailey and I go out in the afternoon."

This past week had been glorious, and a quick smile traveled across her face. "It's been working out real nice so far."

"I'm so glad." His voice sounded like he'd gargled with nails, and she focused on him again. "What's wrong?"

"I would've paid for your furnace. I was going to, I swear. I just got...distracted." He seemed to fold in on himself and then he sucked in a tight breath. "But that won't happen again."

"Graham." She didn't mean to infuse so much tenderness into her voice, but it was there, loud and clear. She stepped over to him and cradled his face in the palm of her hand. He leaned into the touch, his eyes drifting closed, and Laney knew in that moment that he truly loved her.

"I love you, too, you know."

His eyes snapped open, hope bright and beautiful as it shone in his expression. "Yeah?"

Laney grinned. "Don't act like you didn't know."

"Well, all the signs didn't say so."

"Oh, so you're an expert at relationship cues these days?"

He chuckled, his head dipping down in that adorable way he had. "You broke up with me, Laney."

"It was a very hard decision." Laney tucked herself into his arms. "But I wasn't happy. I didn't like how you'd treated me. And I should get to say those things. Doesn't mean you have to alter your whole life, but I should get to have my voice heard too."

"Of course you should. I'm sorry I didn't call when I said I would." His large hand rubbed circles on her back, and Laney enjoyed the warmth from his body, the scent of his cologne, the fact that he was hers.

"Can I kiss you now?" he whispered, his mouth already at her ear and then sliding along her neck.

Laney giggled and held onto his broad shoulders as he gazed down at her. "Yeah, all right."

He growled, a smirk on his face, and then kissed her like he loved her.

———

"BAILEY, SOMEONE KNOCKED." LANEY FRANTICALLY SPREAD another dollop of frosting around the perimeter of the cake. It didn't look anything like what she'd envisioned, but her daughter didn't seem to care.

"Graham!" she heard from the front of the house, and Laney's heart did a happy little flop in her chest. She couldn't believe he'd rearranged his life for her. Couldn't believe he loved her. Then his arm came around her waist, and he pulled her into his side with a "Hey, beautiful," and all her doubts dried up.

"Hey." She pointed him toward the coffee table in the living room. "Presents over there. Bailey's friends will be here in a few minutes."

They'd only invited three girls from school, but they'd

all said they'd be there. The sky threatened to open again, but Laney hadn't received any cancellations yet. She had pizza in the oven, the cake was finished, and even the balloon arch she'd spent the afternoon constructing had stayed up.

"You're a great mom," Graham said out of nowhere, and Laney locked eyes with him.

"I'm just doing the best I can."

"And that's all any of us can do, right?" He watched Bailey as she tapped on one of the purple balloons in the arch. "I have no idea how to be a dad."

Laney loved this vulnerable side of him, the way he let his defenses down when it was just the two of them. He'd always been like that; it was why Laney had felt so close to him growing up.

"You'll figure it out," she said. "Besides, it's not like we're married."

"Yet." His gaze bored into hers. "You know I want to marry you as soon as possible, right?"

Fear struck Laney right behind her lungs. "As soon as possible?"

The doorbell rang, and a shadow crossed Graham's face. "We'll talk about it later."

"No," she said as Bailey skipped down the hall. "Say it right now."

"I don't want to ruin the party."

Laney heard the exclamations and squeals and hurried over to the hallway. All three girls had come together, and she walked down to the door to talk to Allison's mom.

"We'll be done at eight-thirty," she said. "I can bring them back to town."

"Oh, Gina's going to come get them. She'll be here at eight-thirty."

Laney smiled, glad she didn't have to make a trip into town. "Okay, great."

"Have fun, girls." Patricia left, and Laney closed the door, the girls already gone into Bailey's room.

She returned to the kitchen, where Graham stood in the same spot. "See?" Laney said. "We've got time."

"We've talked about having kids," he said. "And you said you'd think about it. I'm not oblivious to the fact that women can't have kids forever." He met her eye, clearly wanting to see her reaction.

Laney had said she'd think about it, and then Mike had come into town. Her furnace had gone on the fritz, and everything had fallen apart.

"No one ever said you were dumb, Graham." She flashed him a smile. "And I know you want kids."

"Maybe just one," he said. "And I could move down here with you and help you run the ranch, and can't you just see it?" He looked like a kid opening the exact present he'd asked Santa for. "I mean, I can see it." He cleared his throat and glanced away.

Some of his enthusiasm drifted over to her, and Laney reached up and ran her fingers along the brim of his cowboy hat. Their eyes met again, and she said, "Yes, Graham. I can see a future with you."

"Then let's get married," he said.

"Those things take time to plan."

"Oh, no, they don't. We send out a few texts and go down to the courthouse. We could do it on Monday."

Laney burst out laughing. "Graham, I am not marrying you on Monday."

Something beastly marched across his face, but he smothered it quickly.

"How about spring?" she asked. "I'm sure the grounds at the lodge will be beautiful then, and that would give me time to get a dress and send proper invitations."

"Celia can make the cake and all the food."

"Maybe you should *ask* her first." Laney chuckled and shook her head. "It doesn't need to be grand. Whatever you want. I've done it before."

"Yeah, but not with me." He grinned at her and added, "I'll get you a ring and ask you real proper." He pulled out his phone. "But maybe we should set a date right now."

She laughed again and threw herself into his arms to kiss him. It was a sloppy, mismatched kiss, but Laney loved the way she felt with him in her life.

"Pull up May, cowboy."

"May?" He looked panicked. "That's four months away."

"It sometimes snows in May. I want blossoms on the trees."

He opened his mouth, presumably to argue, then he swiped a few times and say, "It looks like May third is a Saturday. Sounds like a perfect day to get married."

Laney shook her head. There would still be snow on the ground on May third. "Pencil it in."

"Oh, not pencil." He tapped and studied his phone, tapped some more. "It's in, Laney. Can't be moved."

She shook her head and bent to retrieve the pizzas from the oven. "Go call the girls. It's time to eat."

But he didn't move. "I love you, Laney. I want you to have the wedding you want. Tell me what to do to help you, and I'll do it."

She hugged him tight, intending to take him up on that offer. "Right now," she said. "I need you to go call the girls to eat dinner."

He nodded and went and did as she asked.

THE NEXT CHRISTMAS

G raham stepped into the kitchen, the smell of brown sugared ham and butter meeting his nose. "Celia, you're a miracle worker." He surveyed the spread of cakes, pies, breads, and salads, his mouth watering.

She trilled out a laugh and nudged him away from the candied meat. "Not until dinner."

"I'm starving," he said.

"You think you're starving?" Laney entered the kitchen, one hand on her pregnant belly. He swept his arms around her and kissed her, his happiness shooting toward the sky.

"Hello, wife," he said, a smile in his words and on his face. He'd asked her to marry him on Valentine's Day. Quite romantically, too, in his opinion. He'd taken her and Bailey to a nice restaurant in Jackson Hole and surprised them both with the ring.

They'd gotten married on May third, according to their

plans. Mother Nature had been kind, for maybe the first time, and had held off on the snow until the following week. Graham had taken Laney to Spain, and they'd missed the worst of the snow.

He'd paid off her loan, and they'd hired on two more men to help with the ranch that summer. He loved living in her house, with her and Bailey, the dogs, all the horses and cows and chickens.

When he got up in the morning, he didn't even recognize the man who'd come to Coral Canyon two years ago, and he was very, very happy about that.

Laney had not been able to get pregnant right away, though not for lack of trying. Graham kissed her again and asked, "How's the baby? How are you feeling?"

"Doing okay today." She grinned at him though he could tell she wanted to roll her eyes. She'd done that a few times, and Graham hadn't liked that. He'd finally gotten the courage to tell her he had every right to be concerned about his wife and unborn child, and if he wanted to ask how she was, it wasn't because she was weak or because he thought she couldn't handle the pregnancy.

They'd had several conversations like that over the months of their marriage, and Graham was glad he'd found someone he could be honest with and forthright about his feelings. She did the same, and Graham had taken a few opportunities to analyze his behavior and modify it to make sure she felt safe, loved, and that she was his top priority. Because she was.

"When are you due again?" Celia asked.

"Not until the end of May." Laney eased onto a barstool and reached for a cheddar biscuit. Celia did not swat her hand away, and Graham lifted his eyebrows.

"Oh, so she gets to eat before dinner?"

"She can eat whatever and whenever she wants." Celia gazed at Laney with all the affection of a grandmother. "Are you going to find out if it's a boy or a girl?"

Laney met Graham's eye. "I don't know. Do you want to know?"

"Did you find out with Bailey?"

"Yeah."

"Do you want to know?"

Laney did roll her eyes then, and Graham snatched a piece of sugared ham. "I want to know," he said. "But I don't know when that all happens."

"I'm just barely out of the first trimester," Laney said. "So not for another couple of months."

Someone entered the house through the back door, stamping the snow from his feet. "Woo boy!" Eli whistled and came around the corner from the mudroom. "It is cold out there."

"Wishing you were back in Bora Bora now, aren't you?" Graham grinned at his brother. Both he and Andrew were living in the lodge now, but with Graham's departure for Echo Ridge Ranch, Eli had taken the master bedroom and put Stockton across the hall, with his nanny Meg in the third bedroom in that wing of the house. It was perfect for their situation, and he had a desk in the office with Graham.

Andrew had taken the largest bedrooms downstairs,

and it had a big enough area for his office in the corner. He came upstairs sometimes and worked with the other brothers, but sometimes he stayed in the basement, concocting new events to bring more customers to the lodge, writing press releases for Springside Energy, and basically keeping Graham from having to deal with anything related to the media.

"Nah." Eli took off his hat and shook the snow from it. "I actually like the snow. Stockton is going crazy. Third snowman this week." Eli grinned, a happy smile that made Graham warm from the inside out.

Eli took off his coat and boots and came into the kitchen, taking a marshmallow treat dipped in caramel. "Celia, I love you."

"That's what all the boys say." She let Eli press a kiss to her cheek before he turned to Laney and Graham.

"How's the baby?" If anyone was as excited as Graham about having another Whittaker, it was Eli. Stockton had turned six over the summer, and he and Bailey were inseparable around the ranch and lodge.

"Doing great." Laney put the last bit of biscuit in her mouth. "Graham was just saying he wanted a boy."

"I was not."

"Well, I have a great name for him if it's a boy." Eli gave them a playful smirk. "Eli is such a strong name, don't you think?"

Graham shook his head and chuckled. "We're not naming our baby after you."

"Why not?"

"I think Laney would like to name a boy after her dad,"

Graham said, returning to Laney's side and rubbing his thumb over the back of her hand.

"Or yours," she said, gazing up at him.

Absolute love poured through him at her statement. He swept a kiss across her temple as Meg came down the hall. Her normally short hair, usually cut into an A-line, had grown out since she'd come to Coral Canyon.

Eli practically jumped toward her, a huge smile on his face. "Hey, Meggy."

Her smile didn't come as fast, and Graham watched the two of them with interest. He'd asked Eli if he had any romantic interest in his nanny, but Eli had denied it outright. Still, Graham thought there was some pretty strong sparks there.

"What's wrong?" Eli asked.

"It's my mother." She wrung her hands. "She called and she's hoping to come here for the holidays."

Graham couldn't see his brother's face, but from the panicked expression on Meg's, he knew having her mother at the lodge for Christmas wasn't at the top of her to-do list.

"It's fine with us," Graham said. "I mean, I don't even live here anymore." Sometimes he forgot that yes, he owned the lodge, but he didn't actually live in it.

"There's plenty of room," Eli said carefully, almost in a hushed tone like he'd rather have this conversation in private.

Meg's dark, brown eyes searched his. "She doesn't have anywhere else to go, and now that I'm back in the states...."

Eli reached out and ran his hand from Meg's wrist to her shoulder, a quick movement, but intimate nonetheless. "Invite her. It'll be fine."

Meg nodded and turned to go back down the hall. Graham averted his eyes so it wouldn't be so obvious that he'd been watching them like they were the best movie he'd ever seen.

"So what's going on with you two?" Laney asked, no shame whatsoever.

"Nothing," Eli said, but his voice definitely held a note of mischief and falseness.

"Right," Laney said. "Just like I didn't have a crush on my best friend in high school."

"And look how that turned out." Graham put his arm around his wife's shoulders and grinned at his brother.

"She's my nanny," Eli said. "I'm going to go shower." He left, and Celia clucked her tongue.

"What do you know?" Laney asked.

"Oh, Meg's liked Eli for a while," Celia said. "But that man is as stubborn as all the Whittaker's put together." She gave Graham a pointed look and said, "I'm going to take a nap before dinner."

Graham's mind spun with what he'd just seen and what Celia had said. But he still had the wherewithal to say, "I'll keep an eye on this ham for you," as she walked out.

Celia and Laney both laughed, and Graham sent a prayer of gratitude to the Lord for all the beautiful things his life had been filled with since returning to Coral Canyon.

Especially Laney, he thought.

"Oh, I got you something for Christmas," he said. "Want to come see?"

"How far do I have to go?"

"It's down at the homestead."

The look on her face said it all. So he pulled out his phone and swiped to the picture of the cradle he'd had specially made for their bedroom. He showed it to her and said, "So you can have the baby right by us."

She gazed at the phone and then him. "I love you, you know that?"

"I love you, too." He kissed her and pulled back a fraction of an inch to say, "And I do want a boy."

Laney laughed and hugged him and Graham was so glad he got to spend a lifetime of Christmases with her in Coral Canyon.

———

Read on for a sneak peek at **HER COWBOY BILLIONAIRE BOSS**, featuring Graham's brother, Eli, and Eli's nanny, Meg, which you can read now! Available now in paperback.

SNEAK PEEK! HER COWBOY BILLIONAIRE BOSS - CHAPTER ONE

E li Whittaker stood at the window, watching the snow drift down. While this was a pretty fancy lodge, with all the best materials, he could still hear the excited squeals of his son, Stockton.

Moving to Wyoming was definitely the right thing to do, and Eli was glad he'd done it. Relieved to be closer to family, who could help him with his son, though he had Meg for that.

Meg Palmer, the best nanny in the world—at least according to his six-year-old.

Eli sighed and turned away from the glass as it fogged from his breath.

Meg. What was he going to do about Meg?

"Don't need to do anything," he muttered to himself as he moved through the large master suite and out the door. He walked a few steps down the hall and into the office he shared with his brother.

Graham had not arrived yet, something that meant he was eternally happy with his wife, step-daughter, and the new baby that would be here by summer.

Eli exhaled again as he sat at his desk, in no mood to try to get more people up to the lodge for snowshoeing and Christmas tree cutting. He'd been back in Coral Canyon for eleven months now, and he hadn't had a problem getting tourists and locals alike up to the lodge in the spring, summer, and fall.

But winter was another beast altogether, and Eli wondered if he ought to just take the season off. But as it happened to last for months on end, he honestly wouldn't know what to do with himself.

His thoughts wandered as they were wont to do when he didn't have something big to focus on. And these days, they went straight to Meg and lingered there. Ever since she'd found him late on Thanksgiving Day and told him she had real feelings for him, Eli hadn't known how to act around her.

Someone knocked on the office door, and from the light, hesitant nature of it, he felt sure it would be the woman who'd been plaguing him for months now. Yes, months. A lot longer than just the few weeks since Thanksgiving.

"Yeah, come in," he said, because ignoring problems was Eli Whittaker's specialty. Meg hadn't brought up her crush again—in fact, she'd told Eli to forget she'd said anything.

She entered the office carrying a tray with coffee and toast, a quick, nervous smile on her face. That had definitely changed—the way she seemed so anxious around him now—but Eli didn't know what to do about it.

"Celia asked me to bring you this." She took one, two, three steps, and her foot caught on the edge of the rug.

Everything happened so quickly and yet so slowly at the same time. Gravity grabbed onto Meg, a petite woman, and pulled her down fast. Panic crossed her face and her knees hit before Eli could even move a muscle.

Since she had the tray in her hands, she couldn't catch herself. Hot coffee splashed his jeans in the same moment her elbows hit the hardwood, and then her face.

Time spun forward, and Eli leapt to her aid, his skin bristling a bit at the hot liquid soaking into his pants, shoes, and the rug.

"Meg." His heart reverberated through his whole body, bouncing against the back of his throat. "Are you okay?"

What a stupid question. As she righted herself by rolling onto her backside, pain flashed in her eyes, and she cradled her face with her now-free hand. Tears appeared, and she turned those beautiful, dark eyes away from him.

"I'm fine."

She wasn't fine, and Eli put his hand on her elbow. The simple touch sent fire flowing through him, and he pulled his hand back. So he had a crush on his nanny too and had for a few months now.

But she was his nanny, and he wasn't going to be one of those men who fell for a woman because his kid loved her so much.

Meg tucked her dark hair behind her ear and slid away from him.

"Let me—"

"I'm fine, Eli. I'll tell Celia about your breakfast." She used his desk to support herself as she got to her feet, and she limped out of the office while Eli stared after her.

He hung his head, wishing he could go back in time and change how he'd handled things at Thanksgiving. He'd made a right mess of things between him and Meg, and he was actually quite surprised she hadn't found another job.

Celia arrived just as Eli picked up the fallen toast and coffee cup. "Are you okay, sir?"

"Don't call me sir." He told her that every day, and yet she continued to address him in such a formal manner. It felt weird coming from the woman he'd known his whole life, who used to serve him pancakes at the diner.

"You sign my checks."

"I do not. Graham does that."

Celia tilted her head and reached for the tray. She took the dishes and toast and set them on it. "I'll get Annie in here straightaway. And I'll set more toast for you."

Eli focused on the dark stain on the rug. "How's Meg?" he asked.

"She's...disappeared into her room." Celia turned back toward the doorway. "I'll check on her in a minute."

"I'll do it," Eli said.

Celia gave him a quick glance over her shoulder but said nothing other than, "Stockton's in the basement with Andrew."

"Thank you," Eli murmured, his attention already wandering down the hall and around the corner, past the master suite, to the bedroom in the corner of the lodge where Meg lived. She had two days off every week, and today was one of them. Dared he go and check on her?

"Only if you're going to say more than three words to her," he lectured himself. Their conversations, which used to be so lively and a bright spot in his day, had become stiff. And he hated that more than anything.

In this lodge, with a cook, a housekeeper, a decorator, his brother, his nanny, and his son, Eli felt utterly alone. So lonely. When Graham showed up in the office, he and Eli sometimes talked about something besides the lodge, the horses, or Springside Energy, the family company Graham ran.

Eli had always been able to count on Meg providing a few minutes of laughter, a ray of sunshine. Now, he had hardly anything to remind him what was good about the world.

Caroline.

Caroline.

Caroline.

The name haunted him as he walked slowly out of the office, down the hall, and around the corner. He couldn't believe he'd used his first wife as a shield against his own feelings for Meg.

She'd nodded and clenched her hands together when he'd said his late wife's name on Thanksgiving. "I understand," she'd said, but even Eli didn't understand so he wasn't sure how Meg could.

"Meg?" He knocked on her bedroom door. She had a suite too, though not as large as the master. "It's Eli, and I just want to make sure you're all right." He couldn't hear anything behind her door, not even a sniffle.

He tried the doorknob, and it wasn't locked, so he gently pushed open the door. "Meg, I'm coming in."

The door swung wide and he took a slow step inside, locating her in the armchair next to the bay window, facing away from him. The sniffling met his ears now, and he hesitated. "Meg?"

"I'm really fine," she said.

"You hit your face." Four words. He'd gotten up to four words. He crept closer, noting that her room was absolutely spotless. She was organized, punctual, and practically perfect in every way. It was no wonder Eli had started feeling soft things for her.

With her dark hair and dark eyes, quick smile and keen intelligence, Eli had liked Meg from the moment he'd met her. Four years ago now since he'd been looking for a nanny after the death of his wife.

Stockton had only been two years old when Caroline had died, and Eli spent a lot of time making sure the boy knew who his mother was. But she was fading inside Eli's mind too, and a pinch started in his stomach.

A pinch that would grow, expand, swell until it consumed him. He'd had so little time with her, and he'd loved her so very much.

He honestly didn't know if he could love someone else as much as he'd loved her, wasn't even sure he could love another woman. But Meg had made him start to question all of that, and Caroline had been fading faster and faster since his return to Coral Canyon.

"Can I bring you some painkillers?" Eli asked. "A cold bottle of water? Some ice?"

She kept her face turned away from him, softly crying. She pulled in a deep breath in an obvious attempt to calm down. "I'll take all of those."

With a purpose, he turned to go do as requested. But he turned back to her and rounded the armchair so he faced her. He bent down and ran his fingertips down the side of her face. "I'm so sorry, Meg. Are you sure you're okay?"

She lifted those beautiful eyes to his and said, "I think I'm just in shock, you know? I've never fallen flat on my face before." Fresh tears slithered down her cheeks, and he wiped them away on her non-injured side.

"I'll get your pills and the ice. You can come sit by me in the office." It felt so nice to talk to her like normal again.

She shook her head, agony making her face crumple. Eli wanted to take her pain and endure it for her, and he hated that he couldn't do anything. But he could. Get the pills, the water, and the ice.

"I just want to stay here," she said. "Until I feel less shaky."

"I'll be right back then." He pulled her door closed behind him though her room was about as far out of the way as a room could get. He found Celia in the kitchen with a bag of ice all ready to go.

Eli selected a bottle of water from the fridge and shook four painkillers into his palm from the bottle in the cupboard beside the fridge. "She's okay," he said. "She's going to stay in her room and rest for a while."

"Good idea." Celia flipped a page in the cookbook in

front of her. Eli started to leave when she added, "And Eli, talk to her, please. She's so miserable."

Eli blinked at the older woman. "I talk to her."

"You know what I mean." She rolled her eyes and turned another page.

Eli left her in the kitchen, took the items to Meg, and retreated back to his master bedroom so he could call his mother in private.

"Mom," he said when she picked up. "I need your advice." He cleared his throat. He'd always been very close to his mother, but it had been a while since Eli had needed her quite so badly.

"Advice about what, dear? Is Stockton okay?"

Eli half laughed and half exhaled. It would be so easy to just ask something about Stockton, hang up, and go sit back at his desk.

Instead, he said, "No, it's not about Stockton. It's about a woman."

"A woman?" The curiosity in her voice filled the whole room.

Eli sat down on the bed heavily, his heart feeling as though someone had filled it with cement. "I feel like I'm being disloyal to Caroline, but I like this other woman, and I don't know what to do about any of it."

SNEAK PEEK! HER COWBOY BILLIONAIRE BOSS - CHAPTER TWO

Meg's face hurt. She finally got herself to stop hiccupping, the tears dry and cracked on her cheeks now. She was exceedingly glad she didn't have Stockton today, because she didn't like showing the boy anything but fun and games and joy.

The hint of Eli's cologne still hung in the air—or maybe Meg just had the scent memorized and enjoyed it so much she could always smell it.

No matter what, her crush on him had roared back to full force when they'd come to Wyoming. She'd always had a soft spot for men in cowboy hats, wearing cowboy boots, and those jeans....

Having grown up in Colorado and had several cowboy boyfriends before she left home to become a nanny, Eli now fit the exact mold of the kind of man Meg pictured herself with.

He worked with horses now, too, which was totally

unfair. He had so many skills, and she had absolutely no defense against his charm, his good looks, and now his cowboy hat and easy way with animals.

She'd thought she could be honest with him, that some of the moments they'd shared in the eleven months they'd been in Wyoming couldn't have just been one-sided. She couldn't have been the only one feeling sparks, butterflies, heat.

Could she?

So she'd spoken up, and wow, that had gone badly.

She turned away from the window, wishing she could turn away from her thoughts as easily. "Should've known you couldn't compete with his dead wife." Meg tucked her hair behind her ears, accidentally touching her cheekbone. A sharp pain swept down her jaw, causing tears to prick her eyes again.

She pushed those away too and pulled her comforter down. It was torture sleeping on this side of the wall when she knew Eli was just on the other side. Well, his master closet was, with the huge master bath. And then his bedroom. But he was right there, selecting the perfect pair of jeans and the pink, yellow, and blue checkered shirt that made her throat dry and her pulse pound.

She lay down and pulled the blanket to her chin. The painkillers he'd brought her a half an hour ago was starting to kick in, and Meg felt certain as soon as she woke up from her nap, everything in the world would be fixed.

Another fantasy, but Meg entertained it anyway. After all, she didn't have much else to sustain her, and she often lived inside games of pretend when dealing with children.

She woke, instinctively aware that someone had entered her room. A quick breath in, and Meg groaned and moved. Her teeth ached, and she had no idea why.

"Meggy?"

"Stockton?" She opened her eyes and tried to sit up, but her legs were too tangled in the blankets.

"Stockton." Eli appeared in the doorway, his voice firm. "I said she was resting."

"I just wanted to see." The little boy climbed right into bed with Meg and peered into her face, his eyes so much like his father's it made Meg's chest pinch. That deep hazel that could never be replicated with crayons, with such bright flecks of green.

"Daddy said you fell."

Meg wanted to scold his daddy, but she simply smiled and touched her forehead to Stockton's. "Yeah. But I'm okay."

"Yeah?" He focused on the side of her face she'd fallen on, and she wondered if she had a black eye or a bruise. "Did Daddy kiss it better?"

Eli made a sound like he'd been shot, and he said, "Stockton, come on, bud."

Meg shook her head, her emotions teeming so close to the surface. "No, Stockton. Your daddy didn't kiss it better."

"Should I?"

"Stockton," Eli said again. The child had a knack for tuning his father right out.

The little boy leaned forward and kissed Meg's cheek and then her forehead, missing the sore spots entirely —thankfully.

She grinned at him. "All better." Meg cut a glance toward Eli and found him staring, his hands hanging loosely at his sides. He looked like someone had stunned him, what with his mouth hanging slightly open.

"It's kind of puffy." Stockton touched her eyebrow, and Meg winced away from his fingertip.

"I'll get her some more ice." Eli left, and Meg settled Stockton into her side.

"What time is it, bud?"

"I don't know."

"Did you eat lunch yet?"

"Celia is making it now." He couldn't say Celia's name properly, so it came out like Seela, and Meg stroked his hair.

"What are we going to do for the break? No school or anything."

"Daddy says he's taking me to the movies this afternoon."

Meg had the sudden urge for popcorn. "That sounds great," she said.

Eli walked in as Stockton said, "You should come."

Eli extended the ice bag toward her as he asked, "She should come to what?"

"The movies." Stockton looked up at Eli, but his gaze had locked onto Meg's. In the past, she'd gone on dozens of family outings on her day off. In Bora Bora, they'd gone to museums, beaches, movies, shell-collecting, out on a whale watching safari, and much more. It wasn't abnormal for Stockton to want her to come, and it wasn't unusual for her to go.

But now?

She had no idea what to say. She couldn't tell if Eli didn't want her to come, or he'd just lost his voice again. Was he thinking about Caroline right now?

Meg tore her eyes from his and took the ice, settling it over her puffy eye and cheek. "I don't think I can," she said at the same time Eli said, "She should stay here and rest."

So he didn't want her to come.

Meg's stomach felt like someone had chopped it in half and sewn it back together inside out. She couldn't swallow, and she was about to cry again.

"Come on, bud. Let's leave her alone." Eli held his hand out, a clear indication he wanted Stockton to go with him.

The little boy finally complied, tucking his hand in his father's and letting him pull him off the bed. They held hands as they walked out of the bedroom, with Eli bringing the door gently closed behind him. He didn't look back, and Meg felt like she'd been staked right through the heart.

While she'd wanted to quit when she'd first told Eli about her feelings and he'd hid behind his first wife, she hadn't been able to find anything.

But now...she lowered the ice bag and set it on the nightstand. Anything would be better than staying in this luxury lodge with the man of her dreams just a wall away

—at least physically. But emotionally, he was worlds away, and Meg couldn't keep getting hurt every time they spoke more than ten words to each other.

She got out of bed and over to the desk, the pounding in her head only on her right side, where she'd hit. It radiated from the front of her skull to the back, down to her jawbone and back behind her ear.

But she opened her laptop and started getting the job board tabs open. She could go anywhere, do anything. She had no ties to Coral Canyon, and while she'd only nannied for the past fourteen years, surely she could learn how to scan a gallon of milk and count change.

Anything would be better than subjecting herself to the perfect torture that was being with Eli Whittaker and not being his.

———

THE NEXT DAY, SHE STILL HADN'T FOUND ANYTHING TO PAY her bills, though her face was feeling better. Eli had texted earlier that morning that he'd take care of Stockton that day, that she should go ahead and take another twenty-four hours to rest, heal, whatever.

Rest, heal, whatever.

Those were his exact words. It was the *whatever* that had Meg wondering what to fill her time with. She could only take so many naps, and while she didn't want to be seen with the perfectly round circle under her eye, she didn't want to spend the next day and night cooped up in her room.

The scent of yeast first drew her out of her bedroom to find Celia making bread for that night's family dinner. The following evening, Graham had arranged a Christmas meal for the company, and the next night was Christmas Eve, and Celia would once again make copious amounts of meat, potatoes, breads, desserts and more for the friends and family meal.

Andrew, another of Eli's older brothers, had requested breakfast on Christmas morning, and Laney was making that so Celia could stay home and enjoy the holiday with her family.

Meg loved the family atmosphere at Whiskey Mountain Lodge and her resolve to find another job wavered, just as it had over Thanksgiving.

She went into the kitchen, prepared to say she was fine at least two dozen times. "Need some help?" she asked Celia, who turned and gave her a warm smile. Meg couldn't remember the last time her mother had smiled at her. They spoke four times a year—on Meg's birthday, her mother's birthday, Christmas, and Mother's Day. Meg had been preparing herself for the obligatory Christmas Day call for a week already.

"Oh, just sit down and let me feed you. You're skin and bones."

Meg didn't argue, because it was nice to have someone take care of her for a change. She spent so much time attending to Stockton's every need that she sometimes wondered what it would be like to be the primary concern for someone.

"You didn't come out of your room last night." Celia

set a pan on the stove and opened the fridge to retrieve the carton of eggs.

"I...yeah." Her suite came equipped with a television, attached bathroom, and mini-fridge. She didn't have a kitchen, but she could rinse bowls in the bathroom. "I ate cold cereal with cream for dinner."

"Oh." Celia paused, a stricken look on her face. "Eli?"

Meg shook her head when she should've nodded. "That man is perfectly impossible." Celia flew into action, cracking the eggs with a little too much force as if punctuating her frustration with violent cooking.

"Where is he?" Meg asked, glad her voice sounded semi-normal.

"Oh, he's outside somewhere. Horses or something." Celia whisked and threw in a healthy pinch of salt and a splash of milk. She put a pat of butter in the pan and swirled it around. "I had no idea he'd be so stubborn about his own feelings."

"It's fine," Meg said. *I'm fine. It's fine. Everything's fine.*

"You told him how you feel, didn't you?" Celia paused in her prep and peered at Meg. "That's why you've both been bumbling about with stormclouds above your heads."

Meg nodded, a certain measure of misery pulling through so strongly she felt the air leak from her lungs. "He said he wasn't over Caroline." She lifted one shoulder in a shrug. "What am I supposed to say to that? How can I compete with her?" A woman Meg didn't even know and had never met—couldn't know, couldn't meet.

The front door opened, and laughter spilled into the

lodge. "Please don't say anything." Meg already had enough to deal with.

"Of course I won't." Celia poured the eggs into the hot pan as Graham came around the corner with his wife, Laney.

"Is Stockton outside?" Bailey asked, skipping over to Celia.

"He sure is, pumpkin." Celia beamed down at the little girl, Graham's step-daughter.

"Can I go out, Mom?"

Laney heaved a sigh as she sat at the bar. "Sure thing. Stay wherever Stockton is."

"How are you feeling?" Celia asked, scrambling like a pro and producing a plate of eggs for Meg before Laney could answer.

Meg nodded at Graham and Laney, but she couldn't stay in the kitchen with them. Graham smelled too much like Eli, and the two of them so happily in love made Meg's heart shrivel to the size of a raisin.

And seeing Laney's baby bump…Meg swallowed back her jealousy and loss over what she could never have. So she took her plate, thanked Celia, and headed back to her room.

She'd eaten in her room before, and it wasn't like her mother was at the lodge to reprimand her. The very thought of her mom at Whiskey Mountain Lodge sent shivers down her spine.

She ate with something blaring from the TV and she surfed through the available jobs on the boards she'd subscribed to. It wasn't an easy task to search for a new job. She wasn't sure where she wanted to live, if she wanted to keep nannying, or pretty much anything else.

Her phone rang, and Meg stared at the name on it, because no one usually called her. She had very few friends over the age of twelve, and her former employers weren't the type to call and chat.

Mom.

Dread filled Meg's chest, but she answered the call. Her mother would simply redial every ten seconds until Meg picked up.

"Hey, Mom." She infused as much false cheer into her voice as she possibly could. There was plenty of holiday cheer and charm at the lodge, but none of it had seeped into Meg's soul yet.

"Meg, how are you?"

So her mother wanted something. Meg could tell from the first thing her mom said when she called. And asking her how she was meant her mother needed a favor.

"I'm doing great." She didn't tell her about the fall. It wouldn't matter anyway.

"Carrie's kids have come down with the flu."

"Oh, that's too bad." Meg pulled in a breath and held it. Carrie and Brittany were Meg's older sisters, and they were twins who did everything right. They were ten when Meg was born, and she'd never quite fit into a family that had been complete before she'd even shown up.

"Yes, it is."

More silence.

"What's Brittany doing for Christmas?" Meg asked, because she knew what was coming next.

"Oh, she and James are on that cruise with the kids."

"Mm hm." Meg was not going to offer.

"I'm wondering what you're doing at the lodge. Maybe there's room for one more."

Why her mother would want to spend the holidays with her, Meg could not comprehend. Though she supposed she knew exactly what it felt like to be alone, abandoned, unwanted.

She heaved a great big sigh. "Can you drive?"

Her mother had been forty-three when she'd given birth to Meg, and now, thirty-two-years later, Meg was sure she couldn't make the eight-hour drive from Boulder to Coral Canyon.

Her mom laughed, but it wasn't the happy kind. "Of course not. Brittany took my license at Thanksgiving. I swear I didn't see that tractor."

"You hit a tractor?"

"It pulled out right in front of me."

"Mom, tractor's are *huge*." Meg wanted to laugh, but she knew she shouldn't.

"Can you come pick me up?" Her mom asked like it was a couple of blocks away, that they got together all the time for ham and mashed potatoes, to exchange gifts and sip hot apple cider.

But the truth was, Meg hadn't spent Christmas with any member of her family in thirteen years. The first year after she'd graduated high school, she'd gone to Florida to visit her father. Since her parents had divorced when she was four, she hardly knew the man, and she could admit now that she'd made the trip specifically to make her mom angry.

And she had.

Since then, she'd spent holidays with her kids and the families she worked for. It was better for everyone that way.

"Well?" her mom asked.

"*Well*, I'll need to talk to my boss. I'll call you back." Meg hung up before her mother could say another word. She faced the closed bedroom door, wondering if she should just wait ten minutes and then call her mom back and say, "Sorry, he said no."

After all, then she wouldn't have to endure the holidays with her mother nor would she have to talk to Eli.

––––––––

You can read **HER COWBOY BILLIONAIRE BOSS** in paperback today. **Can Eli move past his first wife and find the faith he needs to build a new family with Meg?** Read now to find out!

Keep reading to view series starters from three of my other series!

CORAL CANYON COWBOYS ROMANCE SERIES

Visit stunning Wyoming for another family of cowboys...
The Youngs! The series includes second chance romance,
friends to lovers, family saga, Christian values, clean and
sweet romance, single dads, equine therapy themes, police
dog training, brotherly relationships, return to hometown,
fish out of water, and country music stars!

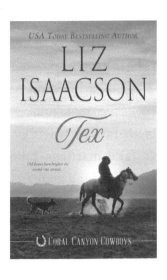

Tex (Book 1): He's back in town
after a successful country music
career. She owns a bordering
farm to the family land he
wants to buy...and she outbids
him at the auction. **Can Tex and
Abigail rekindle their old
flame, or will the issue of land
ownership come between
them?**

SEVEN SONS RANCH IN THREE RIVERS ROMANCE SERIES

Meet the cowboy billionaire brothers at Seven Sons Ranch. The Walkers are new in Three Rivers, and they've got the women circling. Every contemporary romance in this series features a fake marriage that turns to more, family holiday traditions, and the family saga that will create a space for you in the Walker family too!

Rhett's Make-Believe Marriage (Book 1): To save her business, she'll have to risk her heart. She needs a husband to be credible as a matchmaker. He wants to help a neighbor. **Will their fake marriage take them out of the friend zone?**

THREE RIVERS RANCH ROMANCE SERIES

Escape to Three Rivers, Texas for small-town charm, sweet and sexy cowboys, and faith and family centered romance. You'll get second chance romance, friends to lovers. older brother's best friend, military romance, secret babies, and more! The Three Rivers cowboys and the women who rope their hearts are waiting for you, so start reading today!

Second Chance Ranch (Book 1): After his deployment, injured and discharged Major Squire Ackerman returns to Three Rivers Ranch, wanting to forgive Kelly for ignoring him a decade ago. He'd like to provide the stable life she needs, but with old wounds opening and a ranch on the brink of financial collapse, it will take patience and faith to make their second chance possible.

ABOUT LIZ

Liz Isaacson writes inspirational romance, usually set in Texas, or Wyoming, or anywhere else horses and cowboys exist. She lives in Utah, where she writes full-time, takes her two dogs to the park everyday, and eats a lot of veggies while writing. Find her on her website, along with all of her pen names, at <u>feelgoodfictionbooks.com</u>

Made in United States
Troutdale, OR
03/16/2024

18492606R00170